LOLO's light

By Liz Garton Scanlon

chronicle books · san francisco

Library of Congress Cataloging-in-Publication Data available.

ISBN 978-1-7972-1294-4

Manufactured in India.

Cover design by Angie Kang.
Cover embroidery art by Fort Lonesome.
Interior design by Jill Turney.
Typeset in Mastro and 2011 Slimtype Sans.

10 9 8 7 6 5 4 3 2 1

Chronicle Books LLC
680 Second Street
San Francisco, California 94107

Chronicle Books—we see things differently.
Become part of our community at www.chroniclekids.com.

For Finlay and Willa, lights of my life.

BEFORE...

Chapter 1

Summer was like a blueberry pie cut up into all-good pieces. Riding bikes to the pool with Sam and Dante and Eliza. Kicking around with the dogs. Eating dinner at the picnic table in the backyard, all yummy and warm and light until bedtime, which was whenever you wanted it to be.

And there were the missing pieces of pie, too, the homework and alarm clocks and sack lunches. The missing pieces that nobody missed.

It was an easy time, and Millie was happy. But if she were pressed to do that thing teachers make you do on the first day of school—*Tell us what you did over summer vacation, Millie*—Comedy Camp would win, hands down. She loved her improv partner Hanna. She loved games like Dubbers and Who's There. She loved the idea that she might lure Dad to town for the final Punch Line Production. And she loved, almost more than anything, her enhanced ability to drive her sister Tess bananas.

Tess was what Nicola—one of the Comedy Camp counselors—called a Spontaneous Sidekick. "There's nothing like playing off a Spontaneous Sidekick," Nicola would say, and then she'd rub her hands together and cackle. Millie wasn't a cackler, but she had to agree. It was kind of thrilling to always have an act going, and Tess was . . . well . . . the perfect target.

She'd arrive like clockwork at the bathroom door if Millie had been in there for more than twenty-seven seconds. "C'mon. Let me in. It's my turn." *Pound pound pound.*

So Millie would respond, in her best newscaster-narration voice, "The voter stood inside the booth, her hands shaking, desperate to make the right choice, while the unruly citizens right outside grew louder and louder. . . ."

Tess would shoot eye darts through the door and say, "Mil-lie!" Which meant *stop*, obviously. But Millie just couldn't.

"Should she cast her vote for the bath or for the shower? Both would serve the common good."

Tess would yell for backup—"Mom!"—while Millie tried to come up with the next best line, and it really *did* feel like they were in a performance, building off each other and getting funnier and funnier, whether Tess wanted to be—or knew it—or not.

Awash in indecision . . . the tension builds.

No. What about something about a winner *bubbling up*?

Or, *The waiting crowd broke down the door with rubber duckies.*

Usually by the time Millie hit on just the right follow-up zinger, Tess would give up. But Millie wouldn't. As the sister stuck smack in the middle of a very busy family, this was her chance to have a say in things, and she intended to make the most of it.

Like when Tess was talking on the phone and making a sandwich and rearranging her playlists all at the same time. (Every moment was an opportunity. That wasn't something Nicola had said at camp, but it sure could've been.)

"Yeah, totally," said Tess, cheese in her mouth. "Mmm-hmm, for sure." Pause for more cheese. "For real."

Millie reached into space and picked up an imaginary phone of her own, which resulted in more eye darts and Tess swatting at her with the cheese.

Millie carried on, chewing pretend pretzels, whispering into her imaginary phone. "Mmm-hmm, yes. Yes to the yes. And . . ."

Tess slammed the mayonnaise down on the counter and went for help. "MOM!"

"Sorry," said Millie. "I couldn't help it. I can't resist a callback." Technically, that was not a callback—a callback was just a comedy term, one that sounded pretty witty when you were holding a pretend phone. But Millie *couldn't* help it—that part was true. She just loved this stuff. And Tess made the whole thing a thousand percent more tempting by being predictable in every way.

Millie heard her mom in the other room, trying to talk her sister down. Which was also predictable.

"Tess, baby, she just wants attention. Can you give her a little attention? Honestly, you're the older sister. Can't you act like it?" Meg Donally was the chief negotiator of the household, but she brought more or less energy to the job depending on whether she'd just finished a long shift at the hospital. This was a less-energy moment, Millie could tell by the edge in her voice.

"Um, I can hear you guys talking," called Millie. "And, it's not true! I don't want attention. I just want to give the gift of laughter!"

"Well, give it to Lucy," Tess called back, whereupon Lucy appeared at Millie's side as if she'd been summoned by magic.

Lucy wasn't quite as satisfying an audience or sidekick as Tess was. For one thing, she didn't always get the jokes, and for another, she laughed—like, almost too easily—before the jokes were even over, whether she got them or not. If Millie didn't have to work for it, what was the point?

Maybe she did just want attention after all.

"Hey, Luce. Should we make a snack and go walk the dogs? Tess left the sandwich stuff out for us."

"Yes, please," said Lucy, already reaching into the bread bag.

So. Things could be worse. Millie took her time spreading the mayonnaise, stacking the turkey and cheese extra thick, and cutting the sandwich in two. She and her little sister each grabbed a half, called the dogs, and headed out.

Millie walked Boo and Leddy, and Lucy took Hazel, but she was on her scooter with a sandwich in her hand, and Hazel kept zigzagging her all over the place, so Millie finally said, "Here, let me take Hazel, Lucy. You're gonna crack your head open or something." They went along like that, stopping constantly so the dogs could sniff trash cans and hydrangeas and somebody's coffee mug balanced on the curb.

Meanwhile, Lucy tried out some of her own jokes on Millie. "Why did the teddy bear say, 'No, thank you'?" She waited for approximately one second before saying, "Millie—answer me. Answer the joke."

"I'm thinking," said Millie, and she was, sort of, but mostly she was letting the sun hit the top of her head and dribble down around her like a cracked egg, hot and bright. It felt good. It felt like the kind of goodness that might last and last, and somehow Millie knew, even then, to appreciate that.

"Because it was stuffed!" said Lucy, which Millie had to admit was pretty good coming from a comedian who was still in elementary school. She laughed and finished her sandwich and the sun kept dribbling down.

When you live on the North Shore of Chicago, and July turns to August, people start to panic. Quick, wash the dog and the car. Quick, run through the sprinkler. Quick, chalk art, kick the can, s'mores! Fall is coming and then winter and the days are going to get wet and dark and cold sooner than anyone really wants them to.

As Millie and Lucy worked their way around the block with their jokes and their dogs, they were part of this seasonal panic parade. Everywhere they looked there were popsicles and lawn mowers, pogo sticks and roller blades. The Gordons were cleaning out their garage. The Bandolins' dog had gotten loose and

Toby Bandolin was chasing after her, yelling, "Grab her, you guys. Grab her!" And Mr. Acosta was bouncing around their front yard with little Lolo in a baby sling. He waved to the girls and put his finger up to his mouth in the universal sign for *shhhh*.

"He's trying to get Lolo to sleep," Millie said, glad that she knew so much about babies even though it was Tess who was Lolo's official babysitter.

"*Shhhh*," said Millie, holding her own finger up to her mouth and waving back at Mr. Acosta with her other hand, the one full of dog leashes.

"*Shhhh*," said Lucy, pushing her scooter more gently, not wanting to disturb the cutest baby in the history of the world.

"Let's take the long way around, Luce. C'mon," said Millie, with just a little shove to keep Lucy rolling, and they did, and it was egg-warm and perfect. By the time they got home, rosy-cheeked and satisfied, there was no need for cracking jokes or shooting eye darts or special attention from anyone at all.

Chapter 2

It turned out Dad couldn't come to the Punch Line Production. There were a lot of different reasons (which is another name for excuses) including a big thing at work, and Silver needing him for something-something, and also, if he came to Millie's show this week, he'd have to come back out next week, for Tess's piano recital. That's what he said—he'd *have to* come back out. Millie didn't see what was the matter with that. He was their dad. She and Tess and Lucy went to his apartment in the city all the time, no matter what, even if they had reasons to stay home that were at least as good as his.

Sam was over at Millie's house when her dad bailed. He knew how it was because her dad (or at least her dad version 2.0) bailed a lot.

"I can come in his place," Sam said. "It'll be awesome."

"In his place? You're a kid."

Sam shrugged without taking his eyes off the cards in his hand. "So?"

Sam was Millie's best and oldest friend and he always offered to do whatever needed doing, no matter what. He'd do chores with her, or build rock dams in the creek with her, or help her train the dogs, even though they were, according to Mom, utterly untrainable beasts. (Deep down, Mom loved the utterly untrainable beasts. Millie knew it.) Anyway, she appreciated that Sam offered, but she didn't want him actually coming to her show. For one thing, it was kind of for families. That's what the invitation said. And for another thing, there were so many rules about what you could and couldn't say that it might not end up being quite as hilarious as advertised. When they went through the run of show, Millie leaned over to Hanna and said, "Sounds like we can include everything except bodies, bad words, and anything else remotely humorous."

"Wah-wah," said Hanna.

"Sorry," whispered Nicola, like it was out of her hands, which apparently it was.

"Do you by chance have all the spades?" Millie asked Sam.

"Wouldn't you like to know. Are you changing the subject? What's the deal—am I not the target audience for the show or something?"

"I mean, not exactly, Sam, because here's the thing. I think of you as someone who likes . . . actually funny things. Am I right?"

"And . . . that's the game," said Sam, spreading out a devastating hand of cards on the table between them.

"Oh, OK. Thanks. Just when I was thinking you had a top-notch sense of humor, you do something that is not funny in the least."

"Ha. OK, I'm outta here, Mills. I was supposed to be home a while ago. Later, Leddy." Goofy canine ear tussle, fist bump, fist bump, nod. "Bye, Ms. Donally!" Sam called into the kitchen on his way out the door.

"Bye, Sam," called Mom.

"Bye, Sam," said Millie.

"And never mind, Dad," she said to nobody in particular. "The show must go on."

And it did.

First, they did small-troupe improv. Millie's was set in space and ended up being about how she was born to be a star but then all the real, actual stars started butting in and stealing the show. "Oh, my! The glare!" Millie said, when Brandy came flouncing through.

"Yes, that's because I'm a *queen*."

Queen. Queen. That's obviously a hint.

"Yaas, queen! Yaas!" said Milo. (A lot of laughter over that.)

"Cassiopeia!" said Millie, and she threw in a curtsy. There were more laughs then, and a couple of people even clapped. Millie swallowed a bit too loudly. "Well, you may be royalty but I earned my own way here, a lowly commoner who pulled myself up by my bootstraps."

"Bootstraps? Ha! Check out my *belt*!" That was Hanna, strutting around the stage like she was royalty, too.

"Oh, brother. Lemme guess. Orion?" Millie was super glad she'd recognized the reference to Orion's belt. Hanna smiled at her. They were on fire, and the crowd was into it!

After each small troupe (including the one where this guy Rudy talked in the voice of a hamster for three solid minutes without messing up once), the whole group played a few of the improv games that they always played, but this time with suggestions from the audience. Nicola was the emcee and she'd call out to the crowd, "Who can give me a job?"

"Dentist," someone yelled.

"Taxi driver."

"Dog groomer."

"OK, great," said Nicola. "Dog groomer. And a place?" She pointed right at Lucy then, who had her hand held high. "Yes, young comic? Whaddya got for us?"

"Um, I was thinking, like . . ."

Millie wanted to die for a minute as her sister hesitated, but then Lucy said, "The aquarium?" and Millie thought, Yes, good job, Lucy! A dog groomer at the aquarium? That's pretty funny. (And it turned out that it was.)

Finally, after a big, fast, grand finale of Zip Zap Zop, it was all over. Millie met her mom and sisters in the lobby.

"That was really good, sweets," said Mom, wrapping her up in the kind of hug that was maybe too big for a twelve-year-old but

Millie didn't mind. "You were a superstar. The real deal! Oh, my stomach hurts from laughing!"

"Seriously!" said Tess. "And the girl? Hanna? The one you think is so good? I mean, OK, she is . . . but not as good as you, Mills."

Tess pulled her sweatshirt over her head then, before Millie could catch her eye to make sure she wasn't just messing with her.

"I mean . . .," Tess said, as her head popped through, and she shook her hair out over her shoulders. "I mean . . ." But it was too late. She'd already said it. Tess thought Millie was good, and Millie would remember that.

"Can we get ice cream?" asked Lucy. "We usually get, like, ice cream or something, after someone has a game or performance or something, right?" She was right, and they walked to the car holding hands, still laughing about the very idea of a dog groomer giving kibble to an octopus.

Chapter 3

Millie was thinking about it again the next day, as she pushed her scooter down the sidewalk to get the mail, about how funny it would be to see a whole bunch of sea creatures done up like poodles and running around on leashes with their trainers dragging behind. "I guess I'm lucky you're not a school of fish," she said to her dogs as they pulled her toward the mailboxes.

"What are you laughing about, darling Millie?" Mrs. Acosta had Lolo in her stroller and was trying to balance a package on the fabric awning at the top without bumping poor Lolo's little head.

"Oh, a joke I was telling my dogs," said Millie, and it was too nice a day to feel embarrassed about saying such a ridiculous thing. "I can carry the box for you, Mrs. Acosta. If it's too heavy?"

Lolo laughed then too, officially making her the cutest Spontaneous Sidekick ever.

"Lolo agrees with the dogs, Millie. She thinks you're funny!"

Millie leaned down and gave Lolo a googly-eyed smile as a reward, and then she pulled out her mail key and opened their box. Not much. She could for sure carry the package. She tucked some bills and a catalog under her arm and said, "Here. Can I help?"

"You are a treasure, Millie. Yes, you can." Mrs. Acosta handed the box to her. "And actually, I'm glad I ran into you. Tess has a piano recital next Friday, yes?"

"I think so?" Not to brag but Millie was a true master on the scooter. Dogs, leashes, mail, no problem. She slid along next to the stroller as Mrs. Acosta explained what she had in mind.

"We have dinner plans, and we could cancel, of course, but I was thinking you could maybe babysit. In your sister's place. Are you interested in that sort of thing?"

Tess had been watching Lolo once a week since right after Lolo was born. She got to do stuff like that—responsible, important stuff—because she was in high school. It was only fair, according to Tess, although it didn't always feel fair to Millie, who was, after all, already twelve. Still, this took her by surprise.

"Um, I'm not . . . technically a babysitter yet?" Millie said, which for some reason made Lolo laugh again.

"Well," said Mrs. Acosta, "maybe not, but you're a big sister, Millie. That counts for a lot."

Millie liked it when Mrs. Acosta said that because she usually felt more like Tess's little sister than Lucy's big one. She blushed. And then she said yes, thank you, she'd be happy to babysit. It crossed her mind that she'd actually be expected to attend Tess's recital, but she could feel the shape of her excuse in her mouth already—she'd been to a lot of her sister's recitals over the years, and the Acostas needed her. They really did! She could barely believe it. In some teeny way deep down inside, she felt something shift, like that exact moment was the end of her being a kid and the beginning of her being real, full-grown Millie.

When they made it up the hill, Mrs. Acosta took her package and said, "Thank you, Millie. You've brightened my whole day."

"OK, well, bye, Lolo. Bye, Mrs. Acosta," said Millie. And then she said, "C'mon, you crazy school of fish—pull me home." The dogs understood just what she meant. Of course.

It took nearly forever for Friday to arrive, but when it did, Millie was ready. She'd even gotten a solid set of unasked-for instructions from Tess.

"It's a big responsibility," Tess said as soon as Millie told her, and then she kind of shook her head as if to say, *Too big*. But later, sitting at the piano running through her recital piece for the eleven thousandth time, Tess stopped suddenly and said, "So, Mills, thanks for stepping in for me with Lolo. I'm sure the Acostas are glad to have a substitute. And Lolo is actually pretty easy because she's just so cute and happy. Mrs. Acosta will tell you everything, including about diapers, which you probably won't need to change, and she'll tell you where the good snacks are and everything. Sometimes she offers me a soda and I always want one but I always say no, thank you. Mom told me that's what I should do, way back when I started babysitting."

Way back when. Millie almost cracked a joke, like "Way back when, like in prehistoric times?" but she didn't because she was actually grateful for the advice about the soda. So instead she just rolled her eyes a little bit and then said, "OK. And what if something, like, happens?"

"It won't," said Tess. "It never does. But they leave you with their phone number just in case. That's part of the deal."

Millie thought Tess would finish up by saying, "Don't worry," but she didn't, so Millie whispered it to herself as Tess returned to the piano: "Don't worry."

At 6:00 on Friday night, Mom and Tess and Lucy left for the recital. Millie sat at the kitchen table, watching the minute hand of the clock by the phone tick forward until it was finally 6:25 and time to go. She almost grabbed her scooter on her way through the garage, but then she thought better of it. It was more mature to walk to a babysitting job, she was pretty sure. She pictured Tess, with her backpack of books and her jeans and shiny hair—everything just right. So she walked, too, slow and cool as a teenager, toward the Acostas' house—and when she got there, she took a deep breath and rang the bell.

Even doing *that* felt special. Millie often saw the Acostas in their driveway or coming out of their garage or at the mailboxes, like when she'd helped Mrs. Acosta with her package. They always waved and called her by name and asked about camp or school or something, but this was different and important. She'd been asked to come.

"Oh, Lolo," said Mrs. Acosta from behind the screen door, "look who's here! Look who's come to see you and only you!" And she pushed the door open and let Millie inside.

Stepping into the Acostas' house was like stepping into a dream. The curtains were like dragonfly wings—airy and see-through—and the floor and the furniture and the light coming in through the window—everything was either sand-colored or pale blue—you couldn't tell the difference exactly—it was more like a light than a color. And there was music playing softly from some hidden, magical place, and Mrs. Acosta's floaty dress matched everything. Millie felt like she didn't really belong in such a perfect place, but she wanted to.

This was *not* what it was like at the Donallys' house, where there were the two small dogs and one big one and a lot of dog hair and all the stacks of schoolwork and soccer socks, and the plaid couch that was older than Millie, and Mom almost always in her nurse's scrubs—never, that Millie could recall, in a floaty, sky-colored dress. Tess had once called the Acostas' a "grown-up house"—Millie remembered because it had made her own mom a little mad at the time—but she saw what Tess meant now, completely.

"Darling," said Mrs. Acosta, "I'm going to put Lolo down on the floor and you can play with her while I finish getting ready, OK?" When Mrs. Acosta said *darling*, she meant Millie. This is how it was at the Acostas'. The dragonfly-wing curtains and this soft quilt just for Lolo and Mrs. Acosta calling Millie, the big-sister-just-barely-old-enough-to-babysit, *darling*.

"Hello, Lolo," said Millie, and Lolo smiled. "Hello, you funny baby." Millie reached out and did that little tickly, spidery thing you can do on a baby's belly, and Lolo kicked out her arms and legs like she was doing a jumping jack. "Look who's a star now," said Millie. "Queen Cassiopeia's got nothing on you!" Lolo smiled and kicked again and again, with kind of a gurgly laugh to go along with it.

"Lolo," said Millie, taking a break from the tickling, "I like your yellow bird pajamas." Lolo cooed, and talked back, and things went on like that. Millie dangled toys and Lolo grabbed them. Millie sang and made up little rhymes. And Lolo kept smiling and smiling. Millie felt very responsible—maybe even more like a babysitter than a sister.

When the front door opened and Mr. Acosta came in, Lolo startled and looked around and began to cry. Millie reached for her but she wasn't sure if she was the one who was supposed to pick her up or if Mr. Acosta was going to come over and do that. Babysitting when the parents are home was confusing that way.

"Oh, Lolo, you silly little plum," called Mr. Acosta, "it's just Daddy!" When Lolo heard his voice, she stopped crying—just like that—so it turned out she didn't need to be picked up by anybody after all.

"Hey, Millie," Mr. Acosta said as he came all the way into the room. "Thanks for coming over." And then he called out,

"Darling?" and Millie could hear Mrs. Acosta mumble something from upstairs. (When Mr. Acosta said *darling*, he meant Mrs. Acosta.)

Lolo was only four and a half months old (and Millie really *was* only twelve) so the Acostas put her to bed themselves before they left. Millie was just supposed to listen for her and "keep the house company," said Mrs. Acosta.

Millie knew that sometimes they did exactly the same thing when Tess came over. "I got paid just to sit there and do my homework," Tess would brag when she got home, so it didn't make Millie feel silly or embarrassed or too young at all. That's just how it was—the Acostas out to dinner and Lolo in her crib and the beautiful house all quiet and still.

After they left, Millie sat back down on the quilt on the floor and twisted one of Lolo's ring toys through her hands. She felt a funny combination of just right and sort of achy—being here in this living room, wishing it were *her* living room, and then instantly feeling bad about that. She loved her mom and her sisters and her dogs—she did. But she felt different at the Acostas', somehow closer to who she actually might be someday.

Millie wondered if Tess felt like this here, too—not just that it was a grown-up house, but that she herself was more grown up? And she just kept wondering, as the light coming in through the windows got pink, and then gray, and then sleepy blue.

Once it was actually good and dark outside, she tiptoed upstairs and peeked in on Lolo, who was sound asleep, her baby belly rising and falling, a little glistening bubble resting on her lips, her face soft and round and lit on one side by the night-light in her room.

"OK, good," said Millie. "Sleep tight, Lolo." And then she went back down to watch TV.

The Acostas slipped in quietly at 10:15, almost as if they didn't want to disturb Millie, but as soon as she heard the door, she hopped up and clicked off the TV and smoothed out the couch cushion where she'd been sitting, hoping to leave everything just as right as it had been when she'd arrived.

"You're the best," said Mr. Acosta, while Mrs. Acosta counted out bills from the pouch in her purse.

"You really are, Millie," she said. "How lucky we are to have you and your sister to help us love Lolo."

"How did it go?" said Mr. Acosta.

Millie smiled and said thank you and told them everything had been just fine. Then she swallowed and got up the guts to say, "I'd love to sit again sometime."

When she got home, she was proud and newly rich. "I got paid to watch TV," she wanted to brag to Tess. But Tess was on the phone and their mom had fallen asleep on the couch, so Millie brushed her teeth and washed her face, just as Mr. and Mrs. Acosta were locking up, looking in on Lolo—her belly rising and falling—and going to bed themselves, thinking they'd be up again when she grew hungry.

But the thing is, that didn't happen.

Lolo didn't grow hungry. She didn't fuss or cry or make cooing noises into the monitor above her bed. Because sometime between the moon coming up and the middle of the night, when Mrs. Acosta slipped out of bed to see why the house was so, so quiet, Lolo Acosta stopped breathing.

She lay perfectly still in her yellow bird pajamas, one side of her face lit by the night-light, and it was almost as if she were still sleeping. But she wasn't, and nobody knew it—not Mr. and Mrs. Acosta, who'd split a crème brûlée for dessert at the restaurant; not Tess, who'd played an almost perfect rendition of "Für Elise" at her piano recital; not the nighthawks or the raccoons or the nearly full moon coming up in the sky. Lolo Acosta's baby breath had slipped away and nobody knew it, not even Millie Donally, her brand-new babysitter, who'd spent the evening keeping the house company, just like Mrs. Acosta had asked her to do. Keeping the house company and listening to that certain kind of quiet that usually means everything is all right.

By the time the ambulance arrived at the Acostas', with its lights on but no sirens, it was nearly morning, and everything that had been real and true and right about the world the day before had broken apart and was hurtling through the air like asteroids, not caring what they crashed into or what kind of holes they'd leave.

...AND EVERY-THING AFTER

Chapter 4

Tess rarely cried. Sometimes she made other people cry, especially her sisters, but she didn't do much crying herself. Even when Mom and Dad sat the girls down to tell them they were getting a divorce and Dad was moving to Chicago with Silver, Tess didn't cry. She *did* throw a book that knocked over a plant and a glass of water and the glass hit at least one dog on its way to the floor where it broke into pieces, and all of that made *Lucy* cry. But Tess herself did not cry.

So when Millie came downstairs in the morning to find Tess at the kitchen table in tears, it was surprising. Alarming, even. Mom was sitting next to her, rubbing her back, and it took Millie a minute to realize that Mom was crying, too.

"What . . ." Millie didn't have her contacts in so she couldn't really see straight, which made her feel all mixed up and more than a little worried. "What's going on?"

"Oh, god," Mom said. "Oh, Millie."

Everything moved in slow motion then—Mom stood up, in slow motion, and the clouds in the window behind the kitchen table gathered, black and thick, in slow motion. Tess cried harder, Mom stepped around the table toward Millie, the clouds boomed with thunder, and the dogs howled. That's how Millie always remembered this moment afterward—the thunder and the howling and the slow-motion crying people saying, "Lolo's gone, Millie. Lolo's gone. Lolo died."

It seemed to go on for a very, very long time, but maybe it was actually just a few seconds that sort of echoed past themselves. Millie took it all in—the dogs and the darkening storm and the words—but she didn't cry like her sister and her mom. She didn't cry because she knew for absolute certain that it wasn't true. It couldn't be true. She had just been with Lolo last night.

"No," Millie said. "There's no way. I promise, I just saw her last night. I was with her last night and she was fine. Everything was fine, and Lolo was perfectly, perfectly fine! I know it isn't true."

Mom just shook her head and cried and the house rumbled with thunder and then Tess stood up too.

"No, Millie. You're wrong. She wasn't fine. The Acostas thought so, too. They thought she was just sleeping but then they realized that she wasn't. She wasn't sleeping or fine. You're wrong." Tess said all this through tears, so she sounded choky and sad but also, almost angry.

"Wait," said Millie. "Wait, Mom? This really happened? Lolo died? Lolo was so . . . was so . . . alive!" Mom and Tess both shook their heads again, and Mom reached out to take Millie's shoulders, as if she meant to keep her standing right there, in that place, with that horrible, impossible news. But Millie pulled away and her voice got louder and shriller and more desperate. "Mom, are you sure? Lolo died when I was babysitting? Is this really truly true? Is this my fault?"

Millie's mother did not think it was Millie's fault. Not one little bit. She knew that life was sometimes a terrible mystery with sharp teeth and fearsome eyes, that sometimes even perfect little people slip away for no reason at all. But she was crying too hard to say all that, so instead, she pulled Millie back into her arms and whispered firmly, "No, baby, no. . . . This is not your fault. This. Is. Not. Your. Fault." She whispered it into Millie's unbrushed hair, into the soft skin at her temples and the sleepy creases of her cheeks, while Millie stood there wooden and cold, wanting to take it in, wanting to hear the words that would make this go away, the words that would make things right again. But instead, a great wave of noise washed over her, like a plane flying too low, a wave of noise that was a voice but not a voice, that was a storm but one raging from the inside, saying, *Lolo is gone. Little Lolo is gone. You should have stood over that crib like a streetlight, watching her breathe. You should have made sure. You should have somehow saved her, but you didn't, and little Lolo is gone now. Forever.*

And that wave of noise was followed by another wave, and another, and another, until Millie grew dizzy and sick, as if she'd been tossed to shore with water in her lungs and sand in her teeth.

"I feel . . . ," she began, but didn't finish, couldn't finish in the midst of all that roiling, so her mom walked her to the couch, wrapped her in a blanket, and held her tight until the whole world went still again, still and quiet and dark.

When Millie woke from a fitful, foggy sleep, her mom was still there, right next to her, and she was explaining something, something about an investigator. ". . . not because anyone thinks you've done anything wrong," Mom said, "but because when a baby dies for no reason, people are shocked. And stumped. And they really want to figure out what happened." She went on and on about how they'd be looking for some clue, some tiny helpful detail or something—not that would bring Lolo back, of course, but that would help the Acostas understand why she was gone at all. And about how this investigation would, of course, include Millie.

This was another bead in the long string of things that Millie did not want to do or know or think about today. She did not want to talk to an investigator about Lolo and how she should have, could have kept her alive. She wasn't scared so much as sure that she had nothing to offer—no clue, no tiny helpful detail, no answer, except that somehow she hadn't done all that she could have done.

But it didn't matter what Millie wanted, the day kept coming, and when the doorbell rang, she sank deeper still into the couch, in sweats and a T-shirt and glasses because her eyes were too tired and puffy to get her contacts in. Lucy and Tess were upstairs watching a daytime movie on the TV in Mom's room, which was pretty much never allowed except for this one time, and the air in the living room was dark and dank because of the rain outside.

The bell rang and Mom answered it and brought Mr. Sloan into the room. Mr. Sloan said he worked with the coroner's office, and Millie didn't know if that meant he was a doctor or a police officer or what, but she was sure that he would not be at her house interviewing her if she weren't a big part of Lolo's horrible story, this story that had gone so terribly, utterly wrong.

"Millie," said Mr. Sloan. "You were one of the last persons with Baby Acosta last night, so I need to ask you a few questions." Which answered it for Millie—he must be a police officer, the way he sounded all stern and scary and formal. Also? Lolo's name was Lolo, not Baby.

"OK," said Millie. And then he waited, as if it were her turn to answer a question he hadn't asked. "OK," Millie said again.

"Who put the baby to bed last night?" Mr. Sloan pulled out a tablet and started typing with his fingertips on the screen. He didn't even pause to look up at Millie. He just asked, and typed.

"Um, Mrs. Acosta?" said Millie. "And Mr. Acosta?"

"Were you in the room?"

"Yes," said Millie. "No. Well, sort of. In the doorway?"

"And did they put the baby down on her front or her back?" Mr. Sloan still hadn't stopped or looked up. Millie looked at her mom. She wasn't sure if she was doing this right. And she was shivery-cold. Her mom nodded.

"Um, her back. I guess," said Millie. She knew that was right, or at least she thought so, but the whole night was becoming blurry in her brain now, like a dream that you think is real until you're telling your sisters about it over breakfast and suddenly, in the middle of the telling, you realize it's way too weird to be real.

"And then how long was it before she went to sleep? And how long was it before you checked on her? And how long was it before the parents came home? And . . ."

Mr. Sloan may have asked another question, or maybe another ten questions. Millie wasn't sure. What she was sure about was this: His next question, after all those others, was going to be "And how long was it before she died?"

That's when Millie started to cry. Really cry. She couldn't answer Mr. Sloan. She couldn't even see Mr. Sloan. She couldn't see her mom or her own hands all twisted up in her sweatshirt or the tree outside the window, blowing like a sail in the late summer storm. All she could see was little Lolo Acosta, the cutest baby in the history of the world, lying in her crib, a mobile floating above her like a deep breath. And then, through her tears, even Lolo disappeared.

Chapter 5

Several hours went by after Mr. Sloan left—the phone rang a few times, there were a few more cloudbursts. Millie and the dogs stayed huddled there, right there on the couch, until Mom nudged her again, gently, and said, "Sit up, sweetie. Let's get you up and get your face washed. We have someone else coming to see you."

The someone else was the Acostas. Millie didn't know if this was part of the investigation. She didn't know if the Acostas were coming to ask her something or tell her something, if they were coming to accuse her or punish her or cry. She didn't know, she didn't want to know, and she couldn't stand one more thing. Especially this.

"No," Millie said. "I can't do that. I can't talk to them. They can't come. They really can't." The meeting with Mr. Sloan suddenly didn't seem all that bad. He was a stranger, and strangers don't matter in quite the same way. But this—their neighbors and friends, the Acostas, the Acostas coming about their baby, coming *without* their baby, into the Donallys' dark, dog-hairy living room? This was just impossible, and Millie said so.

"I know it feels that way, Millie, and I get it. But we can do this. Humans connect during the hardest of times. We comfort each other. It helps." And that was it. It had been decided, even though it didn't feel comforting at all. Not to Millie.

When the doorbell rang, Mom went to let them in. Tess and Lucy stayed upstairs—maybe they'd been told to—and even the dogs seemed to know not to wiggle or bark. It was not at all what usually happened when friends came by. Millie heard jackets being pulled off and umbrellas being dropped and muffled voices—mostly her mom's voice, actually, saying, "I'm so sorry. I'm just so, so sorry," over and over again. Millie knew that's what you were supposed to say but she didn't really understand why.

She sat all alone in the dark, quiet living room, her face still unwashed, her glasses balanced on the bridge of her nose. She looked around—for what, a way out?—and then she pushed herself to standing . . . she felt that she should stand . . . and she waited until her mom led Mr. and Mrs. Acosta into the room. Mr. Acosta had his arm around Mrs. Acosta. They weren't wearing pajamas, exactly, but they didn't look like the same people she'd been with just the night before. Their eyes were red and cloudy, their hair dark and down and mussed, their sweatshirts heavy. There was nothing light or flowy or well about them, you could tell, and most important, there was no baby in their arms.

Millie took a step forward. Should she hug them? She'd never hugged the Acostas before. They were her neighbors. You didn't just suddenly hug your neighbors, did you? No, they were not reaching out for a hug, so she stopped right there, her arms hanging dumbly at her sides. Feeling this terrible feeling that was already familiar to her, in just these few hours. Helpless.

Mr. Acosta cleared his throat. "Um, Millie . . ."

"Yes?" Millie answered quickly—so, so quickly—without a quiver in her voice. The tears that had come when she'd been talking to Mr. Sloan were gone now. Dried up completely.

"We . . . uh . . . you've heard about Lolo . . . ?" Mr. Acosta spoke slowly and Mrs. Acosta had a blank look on her face—almost like she wasn't there.

But then she suddenly was. In a voice thicker than usual and lower, like she was on the other end of one of those tube slides at the park, Mrs. Acosta said, "Millie, you were there with us. She was fine, right? Healthy and fat and laughing? You saw all that, right? You were there!" She was pleading more than asking real questions, and then, just as quickly as she'd begun, she stopped pleading, waiting for Millie to answer.

More than anything, Millie wished she didn't have to. She wished she wasn't the one everyone was looking at, the one standing in the middle of this particular circle of people, the one who'd been asked to babysit for Lolo the night before. She wished she hadn't been there in that dreamy house with that dreamy baby. She bet the Acostas wished that, too . . . that they hadn't left dumb, young, helpless Millie in charge of their very perfect baby.

"Yes." Millie's voice cracked when she answered. "I mean . . . I . . . that's exactly what I said this morning to my mom. Lolo was fine. Everything was perfectly fine. I . . . promise."

Mrs. Acosta reached up and took her own hair in her hands, as if she were going to pull it all out, and said in that same thick, low voice, "We just . . . we just don't understand," and then she stopped, which meant it was Millie's turn again.

"I don't understand either," Millie said softly, knowing that was the truest thing she'd said all day.

"No," said Mr. Acosta. "No, of course you don't. Of course you don't, Millie. We just . . . we are so sorry to have come. . . ."

"No." Millie's mom spoke up then. "No, *we* are so sorry. Is there anything, absolutely anything we can do?"

Millie just stood there wondering, *Like what?* and, as if they wondered too, Leddy and Boo dropped off the couch, pressed right up against Millie, looked up, and waited.

"Would you like to sit down? Can I make you tea? Or coffee? Could we bring you a meal?" Millie's mom liked to be the one in charge. To have answers. She was a nurse, for goodness' sake, who knew how to take care of people. This was a terrible, worrisome thing that even *she* didn't seem to know what on earth to do.

"No, thank you," said Mr. Acosta. "Unless, darling . . . ?" and he looked at his wife, who shook her head with her hands still twisted in her wild, unbrushed hair.

"I . . . ," said Millie, with only half a heart and half a voice. "I . . ."

"I know," said Mr. Acosta. "We know." And he reached out and gave Millie's shoulder a soft squeeze before walking his wife back down the Donallys' hall and out into the pouring rain.

Chapter 6

Sam was born just nine and a half hours after Millie, in the same hospital where their moms both worked as nurses. He was like Millie's version of a brother, only better. He was less bossy than Tess and less clingy than Lucy and he belonged especially to her. Sam never called before coming over to the Donallys', and he never rang the bell—he just came right in. He ate out of their refrigerator. He attended their funerals (including the ones for fish and hamsters and hermit crabs), and one year he was featured in their Christmas card picture and it was only sort of a joke.

But in the days after Lolo, people did things they didn't usually do. Tess cried, Mom skipped work, and Sam knocked softly on the Donallys' door. Millie didn't like any of these things, and she hated that she could hear Mom whispering with Sam in the foyer and sending him away. She knew the whispers were about her. She knew they were talking behind her back as if she weren't there, as if she couldn't hear them from the next room, and she really, truly hated that. But the part where he left, where he said goodbye and Mom shut the door behind him? That part Millie was glad about. Because she could not face another person. Even Sam. Maybe especially Sam.

Partly, this was because Sam was funny—like, the kind of funny that would've really rocked Comedy Camp, and Millie was 100 percent sure that she would never find anything funny ever again. She couldn't believe that jokes used to make sense to her, that funny felt somehow like an important thing to be. She was embarrassed about that now.

But also, what if Sam thought this was all her fault? What if her own personal, actual, lifelong best friend thought she'd done something terribly, impossibly, unforgivably wrong? Would he be right? Millie didn't think she could bear that. Millie thought it best not to know.

"Sam really wants to come in and say hi one of these times," Mom said after his third time stopping by. After knocking softly and whispering in the foyer for a little bit. After leaving. "He misses you."

Millie shrugged. She didn't know what to say. Did she miss Sam back? Probably. But she was so, so tired, she couldn't tell. She didn't seem to have words or thoughts or feelings anymore. She had worked so hard to speak up, to be clear and careful with the investigator and with the Acostas, but that was only because she had to—she didn't have a choice. It was required, and they'd needed her, and she'd done what she had to. But now Millie was silent and still and she wanted to stay silent and still. As Sam came and went. As meals were served and cleared. As rain fell and fell and fell.

Her mom and sisters stayed, too. Nobody went to work or soccer or swim team. Nobody went to buy school supplies. Nobody babysat. All of them just stayed put, even after the rain finally stopped. But especially Millie. At least that's how it felt to her. Mom and Tess and Lucy and the dogs were all home, but they were doing things. They were home, but they still seemed somehow busy and productive. They talked to each other and they talked on the phone and it was all sort of soft and sad, but still . . . they took baths and showers and watched TV and worked on the computer.

Millie didn't. Millie didn't do any of that.

She moved from her bed to the couch. She tried to eat, but the food didn't taste like anything. She lay awake all night—at least, it felt like all night—and then she'd fall asleep at random times in the middle of the day. When Mom asked her if she'd like to change out of her sweats into something clean, Millie didn't answer *or* change. It was like that. There didn't seem to be any other way.

Then, on the third day, Mom announced that the dogs had to have a walk and everyone was coming. This was called a Forced Family Outing. Forced Family Outings were a thing for the Donallys. They were not to be questioned or refused, and usually, Millie had to admit, they ended up being pretty fun. Like when they went into the city to see that frog exhibit at the Field

Museum. Or when they hiked along Lake Michigan in the dead of winter to look at whole, huge chunks of the lake frozen into sea monsters, looming and wild and white.

Today, Millie knew, would not be like that.

Everyone else seemed relieved that the seal was being broken, that they were being freed to go out into the world again. Tess slipped on her shoes. Lucy ran out to get her scooter. The dogs barked and shook and jumped. Millie thought for a minute that they might just go on without her. There's not a dog in the world who needs a whole family full of people to go for a simple walk, so maybe she could skip it. Maybe Mom wouldn't make her go. That's what she thought.

"Millie, you too. Come on, baby, we're all going." Mom appeared over her and began gently tugging her up, moving her toward the door, nudging her feet into a pair of flip-flops. The last time she'd worn those, Millie thought . . . and then she stopped that thought right where it was. She would do what Mom told her to do. She wouldn't think. She wouldn't wonder. She wouldn't remember.

Tess pushed the front door open wide and Millie took one step. And then another. And then another. She felt like she was one of the dogs being taken out. She squinted from the brightness, even though the sky was low and steel gray. Then Lucy went flying by on her scooter, braids straight out behind her like flags, and Millie realized they were headed straight for the Acostas' house.

Tess had all three dogs on leashes and they were getting tangled up because Boo liked to walk next to Leddy—everybody knew that, except Tess, who never paid attention to what's important—so they were getting all tangled and Tess swore at them, right out loud in front of everybody. Mom didn't even blink. Mom just kept her hands on Millie, moving her forward, like she was suddenly totally fine with Tess swearing and Lucy scooting by without a helmet and the dogs walking with their leashes all crisscrossed.

The old Millie would have cracked a joke about how they were bouncing off each other like basketballs or something, but this Millie said, "No. Let's not go this way. We can't go this way. Can we go another way?" Her voice cracked because she'd gotten so used to being quiet during these long, dark days, and Lucy was already way up ahead, so even as she spoke, they kept walking until there—right there on the right, looking just the way it had always looked—sat the Acostas' house. The big pots of flowers on the front stoop. The silver wind chimes. And Lolo's room—the windows into Lolo's room—high and friendly and framed in eyelet curtains. Millie was pretty sure a light was on in that sweet, warm room, a glowing light, as if there were—right now—a baby girl inside.

She blinked and turned away. She looked through the dark ribbons of her bangs, down into the gray puddles and up into the still rain-soaked sky, and then back up again at the window. Yes, it was true. There was a bright yellow shine coming from deep inside Lolo's room. Millie was painfully glad to see that light, even though she wasn't exactly sure why. Did it mean Mr. and Mrs. Acosta were up out of bed, that they were showering and eating and calling each other *darling*? Did it mean that they were OK? Did it mean (please, please let it mean) that Lolo was OK, that this whole horrible story had been a bad dream and that the Acostas' house was filled with light and music and baby giggles, like it was supposed to be?

Millie reached out, pointing at the house and the room and the yellow glow. Hazel barked and all three dogs got twisted up again and Millie opened her mouth to say, "Look, look at the light!" but Mom interrupted and said, "I know, honey. I know. We can keep moving. Let's keep moving right along." And they did, past the Acostas', past that hopeful gleam, hurrying to catch up with Lucy, who'd already scooted halfway down the hill.

After that, Millie couldn't help herself. It was as if there were a rope of light pulling her toward the Acostas' house, a rope of light of both color and sound. She could've sworn she was being called—sung to, even—and there was an electric answer thrumming in the air or on her skin or in her chest, Millie couldn't tell which. Three more times that day she went out—once with just the dogs, once with Lucy, once alone on her scooter. She still hadn't taken a bath, she still hadn't finished her lunch. But she went around and around and around the block looking for Lolo's light.

"Are you going out again, Millie?" her mom asked that afternoon. She sounded worried.

"Yes," said Millie, "it's not raining." And it wasn't, so she pushed her scooter over the seams in the sidewalk, for a moment thinking it was four days earlier and everything was just right. She was just now on her way to the Acostas' to babysit, to tickle little Lolo, to get paid to watch TV. But no. That night she'd walked, with a sense of grown-up purpose, on the cusp of becoming who she was meant to be. This was different. She was a little girl again, playing make-believe. Looking at a simple light and imagining that it pulsed and flickered, almost as if it had wings. As if it were breathing. But Millie didn't care if it was make-believe. She felt her own breath again, in spite of everything.

After dinner that night, the tinny music of the ice-cream truck rang through the Donallys' kitchen windows, the ice-cream truck bringing up the rear in the panic parade, not willing to give up summer, not quite yet. Millie was the first one to the door; her mom and sisters followed her out into the pink night. There were cicadas, and Mr. Gordon was rolling up his American flag, and Millie and her family moved down the hill together, toward the intersection of Laurel and Stow, where right at that very moment all the kids in the neighborhood, the kids who'd been rain-trapped for days, were lining up for orange sherbet and ice-cream sandwiches and freezer-burned chocolate-caramel cones. Things seemed all warm and sparkly and, honestly, nearly normal. Even to Millie, who at that very moment was looking up at Lolo Acosta's window again. She couldn't believe that nobody was slowing down or pointing or saying anything about what was still and brightly true. She couldn't believe that nobody was seeing or hearing or feeling the pulsing yellow butterfly, the faint buzzing hum of life. It meant something, she was even surer than she had been this morning. It was just too bright and real not to mean something.

"Hey, Mills." Sam appeared next to her as they got in line for ice cream. "I've . . . uh . . . I stopped over a few times. I came by to bug you. . . ."

Millie heard Sam's voice and saw his Cubs T-shirt and the way he bounced his worn-out hacky sack from one hand to another, but it was almost like she didn't recognize him. She just stood there staring, trying to make sense of it all, Sam and the line for ice cream and Lolo's glow.

"I mean, y'know, not to bug you. I was kidding about that. I . . . uh . . . wanted to see if you were OK?" Sam sounded funny. Not actually funny, but just kind of quiet, like not the actual Sam.

Millie wondered if she was somehow getting real and not-real mixed up in her head, but she just said, "Yes. Everything's fine," in her own kind of funny, quiet voice. And then she stepped out of line because she didn't want to talk to the not–actual Sam and she didn't want ice cream or sherbet or anything. She just wanted to follow the rope of light, the yellow song, back up the hill, toward the Acostas' and Lolo and hope and home.

"Um, OK," said Sam as she moved away. "So, see you soon? Like maybe tomorrow? We could . . . hang out? Before school starts and everything?"

"Yep, OK," said Millie with a half-hearted backward wave.

She heard him thump the hacky sack off his foot a few times, and that simple sound was so Sam-like, so familiar, that she almost turned around, caught in a momentary slingshot. She didn't know, really, what she thought or how she felt or what on earth to do, so she closed her eyes for just a fraction of a second and shifted the weight on her feet and then, never mind. She slipped away like a breath, back up the hill until she crested the top and floated the rest of the way home on what felt like a din of crackling light.

Before Millie climbed into bed, she brought the night-light from the bathroom drawer into her room and plugged it in. It was the one they'd had since they were little, the plastic one shaped like a star. It hadn't been used for years, but it lit up when Millie clicked it on, and she was glad. Glad to sleep like this. To keep company with the lit-up room down the block. To keep company with Lolo.

When Mom came in, she didn't say anything about the night-light. She just hugged Millie kind of awkwardly, in that way you do when someone is already lying down and you can't get your arms all the way around their back. "Good night, sweetie," she said. "I love you."

"I love you, too, Mom," said Millie, in that same funny, quiet voice, kind of like not–actual Sam's. And that was that.

Except for the bright hum coming from who-knows-where.

Chapter 7

Meg Donally liked to explain things. She was good at it, always using books and websites and videos and her very extensive scientific vocabulary to fully explain things to her children, whether they wanted full explanations or not. She was a nurse, she sometimes liked to remind them. She was a nurse who knew things, and she was a lot older than they were and she was their mom. They knew all this, but she liked to remind them anyway.

Here are some of the things she'd been explaining lately:

– SIDS, which stands for Sudden Infant Death Syndrome

– Funerals

– The Catholic church

– Grief

– Condolence cards

That last one came up because that's what she was doing—writing a condolence card to Mr. and Mrs. Acosta—and she wanted the girls to not just sign the card, but to really feel what they were trying to express, to really understand the point of it.

Tess didn't even roll her eyes. She just signed. Same with Lucy. Millie did not want to sign or feel or express or understand, because if she did, it would mean that this thing that couldn't possibly be real, was.

That's how Millie felt about all current family conversations, no matter how soft and sweet her mom's voice, no matter how chocolaty the hot chocolate they sipped while she spoke. Millie would rather return to any of the previous difficult discussions they'd ever had in the history of their lives together: How two hamsters they thought were boys could have babies. Why you should include your whole class in your birthday parties. What a nurses' union is. What it means to get your period. Why some parents get divorced.

Even that last one, the one about divorce, which was Millie's least-favorite conversation ever, would be better than this:

"'Sudden Infant Death Syndrome is the death of an apparently healthy infant, usually before one year of age, that is of unknown cause and occurs especially during sleep—abbreviation: SIDS— also called crib death.'"

Millie's mom read aloud from the laptop, very slowly, while Tess picked at her fingernails and Millie looked at the tiny motes of dust floating on the sunbeams coming through the kitchen window so she didn't have to pay close or actual attention.

"Millie, honey," Mom said, "do you have any questions?"

Millie shook her head.

"Did you hear the part about the baby being healthy and there being no known reason or cause?" They were squeezed next to each other in the breakfast nook, which is where Mom liked to trap the girls with all her information and explanations. She pointed at each word on the screen, as if Millie couldn't make out the letters on her own. "Really, honey. I need you to see this. There is no known cause. There was nothing you could have done to change things."

Millie was not sure how that was supposed to make her feel besides helpless, but she went ahead and nodded anyway.

"And Tessie, did you see that part too?"

"Yes," said Tess, before slipping out from behind the table and leaving the room, which made Millie want to leave, too.

Millie knew that Tess wished she'd been the one babysitting Lolo, because if she had been, maybe none of this would've happened. Tess was the biggest sister. Tess was in high school. Tess was prepared and responsible, and responsible high schoolers didn't let little babies slip away. Millie knew Tess thought that, and Millie thought it, too.

Mom and Millie watched Tess leave, and then Mom said, "OK, baby." She took a big breath and waited for Millie to say something back.

Millie wondered if maybe she should tell her mom about the light. Maybe Tess, too. She wondered if it was something they could share that would make them feel a little better about Lolo, but also about her. About Millie. And what about the Acostas? Were they floating in the light like she was, listening to it the way they used to listen to Lolo laugh?

This is what Millie really wanted to talk about—not SIDS, not funerals, not grief, but light. The magic humming aliveness of Lolo's light. But when she looked up at her very practical mom, when she opened her mouth to tell her everything she'd been seeing and feeling, nothing came out. Her mom would never understand it, or even believe it. Millie knew that. She didn't completely understand or believe it herself.

"All right, sweets," said Mom. "I think I'm just going to give you time to process." And then she leaned over and kissed Millie on the top of her forehead, right at the center of her part. Millie felt the soft warmth of her mom's lips rest on her skin a little longer than a normal kiss, as if she were taking Millie's pulse.

Millie did not "process." She did not process the definition of SIDS or the "no known cause" or the fact that Tess surely blamed her for losing Lolo. She did not process her thoughts or her feelings or the fact that she seemed to be losing her voice altogether. She just stood up, whistled for the dogs, and headed out to look for Lolo's light again.

But when she opened the front door, there was Sam—with his hand up, ready to knock in that new not–actual Sam way, sort of frozen in the weirdness of it all, in midair, like a cartoon.

"Millie, I . . . ," Sam was usually goofy, sometimes obnoxious, always funny, but never, ever awkward. Except for now, standing in front of Millie, hand frozen. This was definitely awkward.

"Wanna go for a walk?" said Millie, feeling kind of bad for him. She handed him a leash. It seemed to help a little, giving him something to do, but the whole vibe was still weird, and Millie knew that was because of her. And Lolo.

As they shuffled along, she thought, If I was with real and normal Sam on a real and normal day, I'd tell him all about that night—about the Acostas dressed up for dinner and Lolo in her yellow bird pajamas and the moon rising and what was on TV. I'd tell him about waking up the next morning to Tess crying in the kitchen. And about the investigator and SIDS and condolence cards that got sent through the mail even when the recipients lived just a few doors down. And I'd tell him about the light, even and most especially the light.

Millie really *did* want someone else to see it and hear it, to feel the aliveness of it, and Sam would normally be that person. He'd make a joke to make her feel better but also take it seriously—he had a special skill for that. But not today. Her sister was too silent, her mom was too practical, and Sam was just umm-ing along awkwardly. Millie couldn't tell any of them about any of it. Not yet.

"So, um, do you want to walk over to school?" Sam asked. "Dante says our schedules are out. So should we go pick 'em up and find out what teachers we got and decide if we need to freak or not?" He laughed.

"Uh . . ." Millie stopped to let Hazel pee and then she said, "I mean, you know I love school. I love math and gym and language arts and assemblies and the whole thing, which makes me a supreme weirdo. But the absolute last thing in the whole entire world I want to do right now is walk through the double-dare doors of Montrose Middle."

What Millie *didn't* say was that she didn't want to know who else knew about Lolo, who else had been whispering and worrying and judging behind her back. She didn't want anyone—not the office ladies, not the custodian, not a single other friend—to act even half as awkward as Sam was acting. And she definitely didn't want to receive any condolences of her own.

"Right-o," said Sam, without hesitation. "Let's go down to the creek instead." The dogs wiggled in agreement.

"Yeah, let's go to the creek. Totally."

And just then, Sam and Millie slipped past the Acostas' house without a word about Lolo or her light, which was, yes, most definitely on.

"Millie?" said Sam a few minutes later.

"Sam. I know what you're going to say. But don't." If Millie wasn't brave enough to talk about the Acostas yet, then she sure wasn't ready for Sam to be brave enough either.

So he didn't say what she was knew he was going to say—how sorry he was; she'd never heard so many people being so, so sorry—and they walked the rest of the way to the creek kicking stones and stopping to let the dogs sniff even more than usual. They walked and kicked stones and faked that things were normal for a while. Sam even tried out two new voices on her. The one where he imitated his mom when she was mad was good enough that they both laughed. Like, actually laughed.

When they got down to the water, the dogs started bringing stacks of sticks to them for tug-of-war and fetch. Sam narrated the whole thing with his very best dog voices, probably hoping for another round of laughs.

"Please toss this for me so I can fly through the air like a crazed bat," said nasally Sam as Leddy.

"I promise I will get wet and shake all over you," said deep, dopey Sam as Boo.

Millie tossed a few of the sticks, but then she scooted away and let Sam take over. She loved her dogs. She loved mud and water and this woodsy-sandy beach, where they sometimes caught tadpoles or baby box turtles. Millie had, countless times, waded all the way into the creek in her jeans, because why not?

But today she sat down on the bank as the sun came at her in heavy golden beams, as if it were more than simple sun. It heaved her onto her back and there, right there in the woods under that blanket of late-summer sun, Millie fell sound asleep, her cheek pressed into the pebbly ground, her toes near but not quite touching the water. She slept hard, the sun holding her under, and there were dreams—it was that kind of sleep—fairies flitting and blinking in the woods like Christmas lights, but then the fairies became birds and squirrels and field mice and they were all running . . . no, they were dancing . . . no, flying . . . into each other, into a building brightness.

When Millie woke, it was with a startled cry. Hazel and Leddy were asleep next to her and they didn't budge, but she lurched awake and shook her head and looked around kind of desperately for Sam. There he was, across the creek and down by the swimming hole, playing with Boo and surrounded by a fading circle of yellow—left over from Millie's dream but also somehow real.

"Leddy," Millie said aloud as the dog stirred beside her, "what kind of person just passes out in the mud in the woods in the middle of the day?"

Millie didn't need Leddy to answer. She knew what kind of person. The kind who'd finished the library book challenge and done an improv about stardom and who was ready, really ready, for seventh grade. The kind of person with friends and sisters and dogs and enough money to go to the trampoline park or the movies. The kind of person who'd gotten used to a dad who lives in the city, in a dumb, fancy apartment with his dumb, fancy girlfriend. That kind of person. *Resilient* is what the family therapist called it. Fun and normal and resilient, and finally just about old enough to be a babysitter for the Acostas with their lovely, dreamy baby in their lovely, dreamy, grown-up house.

Until she did exactly that and everything changed and she was falling asleep by the creek in the middle of the afternoon so that she didn't have to stay wide awake with the truth for even a second longer.

Millie wished she could be a twinkling fairy; she wished she could join the birds and squirrels and field mice and fly away.

But as she pushed herself up to standing, she realized both her feet were asleep. She was totally and completely wing-less and numb. Not even pins-and-needles numb—totally and completely numb.

Which, by the way, is different than resilient.

Chapter 8

"Dude," said Sam as the dogs pulled them back toward Millie's house, "you crashed. Like you'd been knocked out or something. That was bonkers!"

"Totally bonkers," said Millie, which must have meant, to Sam, that she was ready for normal Millie-and-Sam conversations again. It was a relief when he talked almost the whole way home about dogs and baseball and school—about how they were going to get to incubate their own eggs this year and how maybe they'd even get to take chicks home and raise their own roosters or something. Sam had the inside scoop on this because his dad was one of the science teachers at the middle school; he and Millie had been waiting for the seventh grade hatching project for a long time. So he talked in a chicken voice and tossed a stone high above their heads and caught it perfectly about a hundred times, and it felt nice. It felt like summer. It felt like Sam.

But when they got back to the Donallys', Millie didn't wave him in like she usually did, or offer to make grilled cheese sandwiches or anything. And to be honest, he didn't look like he wanted to stay. He looked tired and maybe even a little sad.

Maybe if he could see the light, she thought. Maybe the light would help him the way it helps me. But all of a sudden she knew that it wouldn't, because she knew that he couldn't. Maybe, she thought for the first time, the light is really just for me.

"Warmth and light," she whispered quietly. Sam cocked his head to one side and furrowed up his forehead, like he was trying to make sense of her. He didn't actually say anything, he just furrowed.

"OK," she said. "Well, anyway . . ."

And that's when he handed over the leashes and said, "Yeah, OK. See ya later, Millie." It was weird, but she couldn't stop him, and she didn't really want to.

She shut the door behind her, slipped off her shoes, and stopped for a minute to listen to the house. Mom was at work, and Lucy was at day camp, but she could hear the dogs' nails as they ran toward their water bowls in the kitchen, and she could hear Tess on the phone. As she got a little closer, she could make out Tess's actual words.

"It's not technically anyone's fault," Tess said, "but it is the saddest thing. Really. It is the saddest thing that has ever happened to me." And then she paused to blow her nose.

Millie stood frozen in the front hall. *Please stop talking, Tess. Please, please stop talking about the saddest thing.*

"I know, I know." Tess's voice was low and thick like she'd been crying. "She was just kind of young to be babysitting is all I'm saying. That's all I'm saying."

Millie knew instantly who *she* was, but she didn't feel young. She felt old and tired, like in this dark and single moment she was living through a thousand years and a hundred wars, like her night babysitting at the Acostas' had been a long, long time ago. Like she was a character in an ancient myth.

And then suddenly, that heavy, muted cloth of time blew off, and she shook with Tess's words—literally shook—and she went tearing down the hall, so fast and hard that the dogs barked when they heard her coming. She wheeled into the living room, where Tess was lying on her back on the couch.

"You don't know anything!" Millie screamed, and Tess flew up to standing. "You don't know anything at all. Nothing happened to *you*, do you know that? Nothing happened to any of us. Something happened to Lolo, and the Acostas, and . . ."

"I gotta go," said Tess. "My sister is seriously losing it here."

But before she could even set her phone down, Millie pushed Tess with all her might. She pushed her back down into the sinking cushions of the old plaid couch and the phone went flying out of Tess's hand and then Millie hit her older sister—the one who should have been babysitting Lolo that night. She hit her and pushed her, with one hand and then the other and then the other, back and forth, again and again, while she said, "You don't know anything, you don't know anything, you don't know anything," and Tess cried, "Stop, Millie. Stop!"

But old, tired Millie, who'd lived through a thousand years and a hundred wars, could not stop. She could not stop hitting and yelling and blaming herself and blaming her sister and hitting and yelling and blaming—even after Tess had gotten out from under her and the only thing left to hit was the couch.

By the time Mom got home with Lucy and three bags of groceries and, oddly, a soft, pretty bouquet of flowers someone had left by the front door, it was nearly dark outside and Millie was still on the couch.

"Something's really the matter with Millie," Tess said, and she sounded scared. She didn't say, *Millie beat me up*, or *Millie was too young to babysit Lolo Acosta*, or *Millie's bad*, or *crazy*, or anything. She just said, "Something's really the matter with Millie."

Which was true. Tess was right. And as Millie lay there on the couch curled up in her mom's arms as if she were a little girl again, she stared out at the fireflies in the backyard with her swollen, blurry eyes and thought, Look at that light. That's Lolo's light. Breaking up into lots of little pieces and flying away.

Chapter 9

Lolo's funeral, it turns out, was required. A Forced Family Outing of the worst kind. Less than a week had passed but it felt like a million years to Millie, a million heavy years. She shrugged a dark blue dress over her head, stiff and crisp, and it felt heavy, too. Millie's mom was not the type to shop or iron or require dresses on a regular basis or hardly ever at all, so this was just one of the many worrying details of the day. Also worrisome: the fact that Millie was supposed to swallow a big peach-colored pill that Mom had gotten from one of the doctors she worked with. It would help, Mom said, "to get her out the door."

Millie had never needed a pill to get out the door before, but then she'd never been to a baby's funeral before, either. She didn't know what to expect. What if she fell asleep, the way she had in the woods with Sam? What if she cried? What if she had to see the Acostas cry? She took the pill and shrugged on the dress and followed her mom and sisters out the door.

St. John's Parish was a big church on one of the main corners in town; Millie had probably walked or ridden by it a million times. But she'd never truly noticed it before and she'd definitely never been inside. The Donallys weren't so much into church. Mom and Dad had been married in a church of course, and there was a year or so of Sunday school when the girls were little, but Millie barely remembered that. Now her dad golfed on Sundays and her mom caught up on her sleep, so everything about being here in this place and this dress and this mood seemed wrong and unfamiliar, right from the start.

There were two men in suits standing by the open doors at the top of the church steps handing out programs. They looked just like Mr. Acosta—both of them—and Millie thought, Oh, Lolo had uncles.

There were so many things to be sad about.

Everyone wore suits or dresses that had been pressed— much like Millie's—and everyone was hugging and sniffling and shaking their heads. She wondered if they'd taken peach pills, too, and if not, how had they gotten into proper clothing and out the door and into the pews?

As the Donallys walked all the way through the giant, wide doors of the church, Millie felt all the sniffling people with their shaking heads staring at them. Only, not really at *them*, but at her, specifically. The girl who couldn't take good care of a baby. A baby who'd been named, according to the program, Lauren Maria Teresa Acosta.

"Lolo's name was Lauren," Tess whispered to Millie after they'd slid into a long wooden pew about halfway up the left side of the church. "I didn't know that, did you?"

"No," said Millie. And then Tess reached over and took Millie's hand, weaving their fingers together, every other one.

"I'm sorry, Millie," Tess whispered. Millie swallowed a big lump in her throat and nodded, which meant *Thank you*, and *I love you*, and *I'm sorry, too*, even though she still couldn't say that—not even to Tess.

The church filled up and up and up, and the whole time an organ was playing and a bell was ringing and altar boys in angel costumes walked around lighting white candles that matched the white flowers and the heavy paper program in Millie's hands.

She wondered for a moment what Mr. and Mrs. Acostas' full names were. Did she know? What did her mom call them, when they passed each other on the sidewalk? Jess. That was Mr. Acosta's name, right? But was it his real name, or did he— like Lolo—have a fuller, realer, more serious name for times like this? Oh, and Katherine! Katherine Acosta. Lolo never even got old enough to call Katherine Acosta "Mama."

Millie's stomach hurt.

She pulled her eyes away from the program. She shook her head and leaned forward in her seat, staring straight ahead at a gargantuan cross with a very badly injured or maybe already-dead Jesus—his body all bent and pierced, and his head hanging low and sideways. It seemed like kind of an awful thing to have to look at while you sang or prayed. She lowered her eyes a little, to the stage (Millie was pretty sure it wasn't called a stage when it was in a church but she didn't know what else to call it) and there—right there—was a tiny, tiny casket, a casket just the right size for someone like Lolo. It was white with gold trim, and it was raised up high on a fancy stand. Millie sucked in a sharp, dry bit of breath because that was an even harder thing to look at than Jesus on a cross. But then, when she pulled her eyes farther down and closer in, there in the first pew was Mr. Acosta—Jess—the back of Jess Acosta's head—and next to him, Mrs. Katherine Acosta. And it looked from where Millie sat like she was shaking.

That's when it became obvious to Millie that there was nothing to look at in this whole entire church that wasn't really and truly horrible, so she shut her eyes and sat, still and quiet for a moment, in the dark.

When the bell stopped ringing, the organ took a long inhale, and then it started up again with a new song. Everyone seemed to know just what to do. They shuffled to stand, opened their mouths to sing. Millie tripped up onto her feet, too, but she didn't sing, even though the words were printed in the program for Lauren Maria Teresa Acosta's mass, because she didn't know the tune and she really, really didn't know Latin. So she just stood there silently, and Tess did, too, which made her feel a little better. Then everyone sat down again and the priest spoke for a long time using fancy, holy words, but mostly what he seemed to say, again and again, was "Lolo is in a better place now," or some version of that. He stood up there on the stage, behind a podium, in his fancy, king-like robes, and he hardly ever even looked over at the tiny, white-and-gold coffin. He didn't seem to notice Mrs. Acosta shaking in her pew, either. He just stood in front of the very giant injured Jesus on the cross and said, "St. Michael, lead her into the holy light"—Lolo's light *is* a holy light, thought Millie—and "May the choir of angels receive her," and all sorts of other stuff about Lolo being welcomed home.

But when he said *home*, all Millie could picture was the Acostas' house. The Acostas' house, with its floaty curtains and sweet, soft music and baby quilts. And Lolo's room—her nursery at the top of the stairs—pulsing and humming and breathing with light. That's what Millie pictured, while everyone else listened and sat and kneeled and prayed and stood and sang again.

"Lord of all gentleness, Lord of all calm,
whose voice is contentment, whose presence is balm:
Be there at our sleeping, and give us, we pray,
Your peace in our hearts, Lord, at the end of the day."

When the last note from the organ faded away, you could hear sniffling in the church. Millie put her hand up to her heart to see if it was racing, and then to her cheeks to see if they were wet with tears. But the peach pill that had helped get her out of the house made it so she wasn't racing or crying. She was just dreaming.

Or maybe this wasn't a dream at all, maybe it was all real. Could it be real? The waves of light rising up from the tiny coffin, spilling out onto the street, beaming through Lolo's window and pouring off Millie's little plastic star as she fell asleep that night. Was Lolo's light alive?

Chapter 10

Once you hit seventh grade, you're not middle school rookies anymore. You know your way around already, you know the teachers, you know how to ace a test. It's not like high school or anything—Tess says high school is "the real deal"—but still, Millie had been looking forward to the grown-up grandness of seventh grade for a long time.

Until suddenly she wasn't looking forward to anything at all.

Sam had tried again, a couple of times, to talk her into picking up their schedules. Once, the day after the funeral, they'd gone to the mini-mart right around the corner from school and he'd waved his hands in front of her eyes, saying, "C'mon! Aren't you dying to see into the future?" And a few days earlier he'd said, "It's your solemn duty to prepare yourself," using a very thick British accent. But Millie was immune to his humor and charm. Instead, they'd gone back to the creek for another, less-sleepy run with the dogs, and Sam had beaten her in a rock-skipping contest. Millie was usually the skipping champ, so he called this an "epic win." They'd gone to the grocery store for molasses cookie ingredients. They'd made molasses cookies. They'd eaten molasses cookies until they both felt sick. And they'd walked by the Acostas' house, with its glowy yellow windows, at least ten times.

What they hadn't done was pick up their schedules. Or gotten their lockers or gym uniforms. Or accidently bumped into anyone else who might be doing any of those things, aka their friends.

Today, though, was unavoidable, and Millie knew it. She saw it in her mom's eyes across the breakfast table. She saw it in the sack lunches and backpacks by the door. And she saw it on the great big family calendar, in Meg Donally's hurried, nurse's scrawl—the cold, hard truth about today:

1st day of school

It was something Millie knew she had to do and also something she knew she simply couldn't. Tess nudged her out the door and walked down the hill with her, talking the whole way about some big issue in her friend group. It was very complicated and didn't require Millie's input, which Millie appreciated. They parted ways in the parking lot—Tess turning toward the high school, Millie trudging toward the middle school, past the flagpole, until there was Sam, waiting for her by the big front doors. He had both their schedules, and he waved hers like a winning ticket.

"Look!" he said. "Great news! Let's go!"

"OK," said Millie. She heard the surprise in her own voice.

Was she almost a little bit excited all of a sudden? "Thanks," she said, taking the piece of paper from Sam's hands. It was the first day of school. The first day of seventh grade!

Then she looked through the double glass doors at all the millions of middle schoolers pushing and shouting and looming, and she thought, No way. There is absolutely no way.

"Ready?" Sam said. "We've both got Brustein for homeroom." Which meant Millie didn't have to look at her schedule, or find the right room, or sit next to kids who weren't Sam, or anything.

So she nodded and said, "Yep, ready. Cool. Thanks," as if saying things were cool would make them cool. Sam smiled and led the way.

Millie thought it was going to be like walking into St. John's Parish the day of so-called Lauren Acosta's funeral—everyone looking at her, even that badly injured Jesus on his giant cross. But here's the thing about people: Most of the time they're busy thinking about and looking at and discussing *other* things—not the stuff you think they're looking at and thinking and talking about. So when Millie walked into Montrose Middle School, the world did not stop spinning. People did not stop walking or talking. They did not stare. They were trying to figure out which room to go to. They were fist-bumping and laughing and high-fiving and *hey, dude*-ing. They were thinking, I'm looking good. Aren't I? I think I am. I'm looking good. They were trying to beat the bell. It was . . . normal.

Millie stood up a little straighter. She skimmed along the locker lane, keeping Sam solid as a soldier on her left side, all the way to Mr. Brustein's homeroom, and then she sank into a seat in the second row before anyone could even notice she was there.

That's when the bell rang and the allegiance got pledged and the class quieted down and Mr. Brustein asked the most original question ever.

"So. Gang. What did you guys do over summer vacation? Shall we go around? Let's go around." He pointed at Luisa, thank goodness, because Luisa really, really knew how to talk.

"Well," Luisa started. "OK, let me keep this short and sweet. If I can. Aaaack, I mean, I did a lot this summer. Because, y'know, my dad is an airline pilot. . . ."

Millie didn't look around but she imagined everyone rolling their eyes and groaning because yes, they all knew that Luisa's dad was a pilot. Once you've been told something one hundred thousand times, you just knew it. It was fact.

Luisa kept going. Mexico, blah blah, Los Angeles, blah blah. Grandparents, a musical, an archeological dig, blah blah blah. Mr. Brustein finally cut her off and Millie knew that in exactly five turns, if he went up and down the rows in order, it would be her turn. She would have to say, in front of everyone, what she did this summer.

She squinted her eyes against the sun pouring in through the wide bank of windows, and she pressed her hands into her ears so the buzzing from the overhead lights disappeared, so Marcus and Courtney and Michael and Sam disappeared. She took in a long, deep breath and the sunlight turned white and blue and orange in her eyes, and she whispered, "Lolo."

"What's that, Ms. Donally?" said Mr. Brustein. And he meant it nicely, Millie could tell, but now everyone really was looking at her, just like she'd expected.

"Um, I went to comedy camp," she said. Only it sounded like "Um, I went to comedy camp?" Like it was a question, like she was asking Mr. Brustein instead of telling him. Like she was saying, *Mr. Brustein, can I please have permission to tell you about this single dumb, inconsequential thing instead of telling you the worst possible story about the best possible baby in the whole wide world?*

"Oooooh, comedy camp," said Mr. Brustein. "I've got a bit of a funny bone myself," which meant, yes, Millie had permission. At least from him.

"Is that it?" someone fake-whispered from a few rows over.

"Yes, that's it," said Millie, but what she thought was, Everybody knows. Everybody knows. Everybody knows about Lolo. She squeezed her eyes shut again, just for a second, and wished that they also knew about the light. She wished she could tell them about how Lolo—some part of Lolo—was still here, in the world, in some weird way. And without even meaning to, she pressed her hands onto her desk and started to stand, so desperate was this urge to defend herself, so pressing was this desire to explain this thing both magical and true.

There was an audible suck of breath as she began to stand—it was everybody's breath—and she heard someone say, "Dude, what?" which broke the spell. Millie sank back down and looked intently at Sam in the next seat over, like she was passing a ball to him, and he caught it.

"OK, yeah, so I'm up next," he said. Because he was absolutely perfect.

The whole day kind of went like that. Nobody actually ever said, "Hey, Millie, we heard what happened, about how you were babysitting and you couldn't even keep the baby alive." But it was just there in the air—Lolo herself was just there, all the time.

Is this how it is for Mrs. and Mr. Acosta? Millie wondered. Is Lolo always there, every minute, like this huge balloon in the chest, like this canyon of echoey space that you walk with and through? Millie knew she must be. She knew she was.

It was exhausting, honestly. It was only lunchtime and Millie felt like 100 hours had gone by. "Millie," said Sam, "are you gonna eat those?" Millie never ate tater tots. French fries, yes. Tater tots, with their weird, ricey texture? Um, NO. Sam knew that, but he always asked before helping himself anyway.

"Who in the world doesn't like tater tots?" asked Eliza as she and Sam dug in.

"Millie doesn't," said Sam with his mouth full, which made Millie smile. As if Sam had gone to bat for her in a big way, in a way that was bigger than just defending her choice of processed potato product.

"OK, so let's compare schedules. Who's got what after lunch?" Eliza pulled a piece of paper from her pocket and pressed it flat on the table in front of her. So did Bonnie and Anna and Dante.

"Oh, by the way," said Anna, "I got your dad, Sam. I'm psyched. You can put in a good word for me! Did you get him, too?"

"Nope. Conveniently, there's a rule against that," said Sam. "Millie and I both got Ms. Fritz." Which is when Millie fully understood that Sam had her schedule memorized and was officially the only reason she was making it through this impossible and endless day. She popped up a fist for a bump and he answered with one, without even totally knowing what it was for.

"Oh, you did? Awesome," said Eliza. "I got her, too. I'm with you guys! Let's go. The bell's about to ring."

And sure enough the cafeteria flew to life, like when a flock of birds all take off at once, with one wild, feathery scream. The plastic trays clattered, the silverware splashed into big, gross, watery tubs, the bell rang. Millie blinked and followed closely behind Sam as he maneuvered his way through the birds, the clattering, the splashing, the ringing. But somewhere in there, woven through the chaos of the cafeteria, was a delicate thread of golden light—speaking, no, *singing* directly to Millie.

"Lolo," Millie answered.

Chapter 11

"So, because the seventh-grade gossip grapevine is strong and lively, I presume you all already know that we build our first-semester science curriculum around an egg-hatching project, right?" Ms. Fritz had all the desks arranged in two semicircles, like a little rainbow, and she sat on a table at the front, swinging her feet. She looked, honestly, all pumped up. Like a coach before a big game. Even though she did this exact same thing every single year. Her eyes were shiny, and her feet swung, and she acted like she loved nothing more than eggs. And incubators. And baby chicks. Year after year. Over and over and over again. "So get ready, my friends! Because seventh-grade science is just an awesome adventure!"

And it was in that very moment—in the pause between Ms. Fritz's words leaving her mouth but before they actually reached the two smiling semicircles of seventh graders—that Millie realized this:

They were about to embark on months of birthing and babysitting tiny, tender, fragile little creatures who would be completely dependent on them. If that wasn't the most absurd twist of fate.

"Excuse me," Millie blurted as she jumped up and kicked free from her desk, knocking the whole thing over onto Aisha. Aisha cried out, but Millie didn't even pause—not to apologize, not to help her classmate out from under the heavy desk.

She heard Sam say, "Millie, what . . ." But by then she was flying through the door and out into the echoey emptiness of Montrose Middle School when class was in session. And there, waiting like a promise, was the wheeled custodian's cart with its huge trash can—floating, unattended, in the middle of the hallway. It's a good thing, too, because Millie wasn't anywhere close to making it to the restroom on time.

She was leaning against the lockers, breathing, recovering, when Ms. Fritz peeked out to check on her. "Oh, Millie, you poor thing! To be sick on the first day of school! Listen—you go ahead to the restroom and then maybe to the nurse's office. You can rest in there. Your group will fill you in on what we talk about. It's just basic prep. You won't miss a thing."

Millie headed toward the bathroom to rinse out her mouth and splash her face. She looked at herself in the mirror, all blurry and distorted, and felt sick all over again. She should've gone to the nurse's next—that's what Ms. Fritz had said to do—but she couldn't think of anything worse than having to wait out the day on a sweaty plastic cot with a nurse who wasn't her mom. Millie was picky about her nurses.

Instead, she turned the other direction and slipped into the library where she found herself face-to-face with a sprawling display of—you could not make this up—*The Baby-Sitters Club* graphic novels. Next to a sign for a Red Cross babysitting class being held this weekend.

Millie felt her cheeks heat up and her mouth get sticky. "Seriously?" She reached out and grabbed hold of the top of the nearest bookshelf. She tried to steady herself. She actively tried to hold herself up, to avoid tumbling onto the carpet like a stack of blocks. "Seriously?" she said again.

The librarian interrupted. "Looking for anything special?" She walked over to Millie with a smile on her face. She was new this year, and Millie did not know her name.

"I just . . . I was looking for a place to sit down," Millie said.

"Oh," said the librarian. "Well, perfect. Me too." And she waved her hand toward the tables in the center of the room. Millie slipped into a chair and put her head down on the table. She thought it was possible, if she didn't throw up again, that she might fall into one of those weird, woodsy sleeps, like she had with Sam. The librarian disappeared into her little glass office and reemerged with hummus and a giant bag of pretzels.

"I'm Ms. Marion. The librarian," she said. "Which I know is funny or ridiculous or whatever, but that's what they called me when I was born—Marion—long before I'd ever stepped into a library." She smiled again, or maybe she had never stopped. "Hummus?"

"Uh, sure? Thanks," Millie said, hoisting herself back up onto her elbows. "I'm Millie."

"Excellent. Lovely," said Marion the librarian. She poured a whole pile of pretzel twists onto the table. "So Millie, I was just settling in to read a little. What about you?"

Millie could have hugged her then, even though they'd just met. She understood that Ms. Marion was letting something slide. She didn't know why. She didn't know why she wasn't being sent back to class, but all that mattered was that there would apparently be no questions, no excuses, and no conversation, which was just what she wanted.

"Uh, yes. Yes! Sounds good," she said, and she got up to look for a book of her own.

But all the wrong things kept jumping out at her. Ghost stories. Survival guides. Something called *Sisters*, which she had more than enough of at home, thank you very much. So she headed over to the nonfiction animal section, because that was usually a safe bet, and there—somewhere near arachnids and not too far from chickens—was a book about bioluminescence. The title, *The Magic of Bioluminescence*, was in raised letters on the shiny, pearlized cover, and the words were surrounded by pictures of fireflies and jellyfish. She was pretty sure the whole thing would've glowed in the dark if Ms. Marion suddenly flicked off the lights.

Millie opened the book as she walked back to the table where Ms. Marion sat, chewing rhythmically and already lost in her own reading. Inside, there were pages and pages of pictures. Glow-in-the-dark pictures of glow-in-the-dark things. More fish. Mushrooms. Glowworms.

"The light can be used to lure prey," said the book.

". . . to attract mates," said the book.

". . . to warn, to signal, to communicate," said the book.

"Lolo," whispered Millie, not caring if Ms. Marion the librarian heard her or not.

"Enzymes . . . luciferase . . . cofactors," said the book. Millie read and reread, from the middle and both backward and forward, quickly, in fits and starts, the words and pictures peppering her eyes like little pinpricks of, well, light. The hands flew around the library clock and she turned page after page. Ms. Marion got up twice, first to get a stack of paperwork and then to get her laptop, but Millie kept reading.

And then finally, she stopped. She read the last bit again. And again. Then she read it out loud. "'At its most simplistic level, bioluminescence can be understood as light that is both produced and emitted by a living organism.'"

"Interesting!" said Ms. Marion.

"Lolo," said Millie. She grabbed a couple of pretzels, walked directly over to the checkout counter to scan the book, and said, "Thanks, Ms. Marion," before making her way back into the sea of middle school humanity.

Chapter 12

Sam was waiting out by the flagpole when the last bell rang. "So, Ms. Fritz says the first thing we're going to do is build our own brooding boxes," he said, as if Millie'd just slipped out of class for a minute instead of losing her entire lunch in a trash can and disappearing for the rest of the day. "And we get to pick our own groups. So that's great, right? We get to work together. You and me and Eliza."

"Yeah, that is," said Millie. Her mind was still on enzymes, luciferase, cofactors.

"That is what?" said Sam.

"Great. That is great," said Millie. "That we get to be together, I mean." She knew she didn't sound wildly enthusiastic, but she *was* relieved. She felt sure she would not survive a single moment with a brooding box, an egg, or a real, live chick if not for Sam. Even *with* Sam, things had gotten off to a pretty bumpy start.

"Yeah, my dad is stricter than Ms. Fritz. He assigns groups. We got put in the right class, for sure. Want a soda?" He cut in front of Millie to go into the mini-mart around the corner from school. They usually went in together, debated soda vs. ice cream vs. chips vs. candy—serious, high-level decision-making—but she just sort of froze in place today, hoping nobody she knew walked by.

Millie knew that Sam was joking about his dad. Mr. Clark was top-notch—everyone thought so. He'd been Tess's science teacher when she was in seventh grade, and she still said he was one of her favorites. (Which was saying something. Tess didn't have a lot of favorites.) These days, Millie thought any dad who stuck around instead of running off to live in the city with a dumb, fancy girlfriend was top-notch, even if he was a teacher and a tiny bit strict.

The mini-mart door dinged, and Sam reappeared with a couple cans of ginger ale.

"I thought this would be good for the flu. Or, whatever you've got. Is it the flu?" he asked.

Three older kids on skateboards came straight toward them then, fast, and Sam hopped off the sidewalk while Millie scootched back toward the building.

"Dudes," said Sam when they'd passed. "Not cool."

"It's not the flu," said Millie, as the skaters' wheels rattled away. She started walking again, faster now. Sam stepped back onto the sidewalk and caught up with her, the afternoon sun overhead, their shadows long on the sidewalk.

"It's not?"

"No," said Millie. She wanted to look at Sam, but she couldn't. She knew if she did, she'd never say what needed saying. "No, it's Lolo."

"Oh," said Sam. "Yeah. Yeah, I get that." And they walked a little farther, a little more deeply into their shadows, sipping their ginger ales.

"I'm sorry," Sam said then, after a long stretch of seconds. "Seriously, I'm really sorry about all that, Millie. What a weird, super-duper sad thing." And then, after another sip and a pause, he said, "Everybody knows it wasn't your fault. You know that, right?"

Millie didn't know that. All she knew was that at the top of this hill on the left-hand side sat the Acostas' house, and if anything at all was still right with the world, Lolo's light would be on when they passed.

"Thanks, Sam. Seriously. But also, I have to . . . I have to tell you something." Millie looked down at her feet in her too-small sneakers. The back-to-school shopping never happened this year, because of Lolo and everything, so she was in too-small sneakers, taking one slow step at a time toward home.

"Um, OK," said Sam. "What's up?"

"You're not going to believe me," said Millie.

"How do you know?" Sam was listening, but he was also tossing his now-empty soda can in the air overhead and catching it and tossing it and catching it and kicking it and catching it.

Millie was fine with the distraction.

"I sort of don't think Lolo's really exactly gone." There. She'd said it. It was somehow ridiculous but also not, and she'd said it out loud to Sam.

Sam caught the can. He stopped tossing and kicking and walking. He just stood there looking at Millie. "Um, OK," he said. He didn't move an inch. He didn't even blink. He looked hard at her, maybe waiting for her to laugh. Or cry. Or say, *Only kidding, Sam.* She didn't.

"Um, what do you mean?" he asked.

"I mean, some part of her is still here, on Earth. I'll show you." And she started walking again.

Sam followed Millie, one step, then another, and another, and another. Until right there, on their left, was the Acostas' house. The flowerpots, the wind chimes, the light.

"Do you see it?" Millie asked Sam. "Do you see the yellow light coming through that window?" Millie put one hand on Sam's arm, and with the other hand, she pointed up at what was so obvious to her.

Sam nodded. "Yeah?"

"That's Lolo," she said. "I mean . . . sort of," she said.

"Um, OK," said Sam. "Hmm." He did not sound sure at all. In fact, she heard that weird awkwardness in his voice again, like she had the first few times they'd seen each other after everything.

She wanted to explain bioluminescence to him, she wanted to tell him how Lolo somehow *was* the light but how she was also making the light, the light that was capable of pulling Millie along through these days like a familiar song. She wanted Sam to believe it, to help her believe it herself, but she didn't know what else to say to make it real or true.

"Yeah, well, OK," she said, and she just started walking again, releasing them both from having to say another word.

Chapter 13

Today they'd start their hatching project in earnest. Millie sat on her hands and listened as Ms. Fritz explained how the rest of the fall would be divided up into segments that emphasized different kinds of science—structural and electrical engineering, genetics, life science, chemistry—so they could learn about cells and matter and heat transfer and sustainability, all using chicken eggs. "Whole science," she called it. "Experiential, whole science!" She was almost glistening when she said this, and Millie, without meaning to, got the teensiest bit excited herself.

Building brooding boxes was the first step, the engineering part. Some groups would work with wood, others might use Styrofoam or cardboard or sheet metal.

"Last year," said Ms. Fritz, "one group retrofitted an old-fashioned TV cabinet!" She seemed impressed by that. "And another," she said, "used a plastic storage bin, pretty much as is." Which was obviously less impressive, to Millie and to Ms. Fritz.

Millie, Sam, and Eliza were a group. Eliza wanted to use plywood. Sam thought cardboard might be easier.

"It's not about what's easier," said Eliza. "It's about what's best. For the chickens. Or for the eggs, at least. Right, Millie?"

Usually, Eliza would be able to count on Millie for backup when it came to school stuff—they both knew that, and so did Sam—but the truth was, Millie didn't *know* what was best. Her momentary excitement dwindled. The graph paper in front of her lay still and plain.

"Millie, seriously. Weigh in on this. You're hardly saying anything!" Eliza sounded annoyed.

Millie'd never built a brooding box. She'd never hatched an egg. She'd never raised a chick. She wanted to help her team, but she sat there frozen and scared. Why wasn't Ms. Fritz giving better instructions? Millie didn't know how to answer Eliza. She didn't know what to do.

"OK...um..." Millie's mind raced. What could she say? Why were Sam and Eliza looking at her like she had answers? What if she didn't want to be the one to decide, to be in charge, to determine what was best for these chicks?

"Dude, Liza, no biggie," said Sam, but Eliza was having none of that.

"Yes, biggie. Yes! This is the beginning of our whole huge project, and Millie's smart," said Eliza. "Come on, what do you think the eggs need, Millie?"

"OK," Millie said again. And then, almost without thinking, she said, "Warmth and light."

"Millie...!" Eliza spoke through gritted teeth. She looked like she wanted to scream.

"Eliza, give it a rest, will you?" Sam was trying to help, but Millie understood that Eliza needed more from her.

"OK, I don't know if it matters if we use wood or cardboard," Millie said, "as long as we figure out a way to give them lots of warmth and light." And then she drew a giant circle—a sun, really—in the middle of her graph paper, knowing deep down that what she'd said was true but also no help at all. Eliza just wanted her vote.

"OMG. Millie," said Eliza, shaking her head. "OK, I *will* give it a rest, *if* we can use plywood for our brooding box. Deal?"

"Deal," said Sam and Millie at the same time.

"Excellent, awesome," said Eliza, rolling her eyes. "Now, can we up our game?"

Sam jumped back in without rolling a single eyeball. "Yep, all the way up," he said. "This is gonna be fun, you guys. Seriously. Let the schematics begin!"

Sam was more than resilient. He was like a human spring, a human bungee jump. He recovered so quickly and completely that they *all* did. Eliza was laughing again, and Millie was breathing.

For the rest of the week, the three of them pretty happily measured and calculated and drew and erased and crumpled up and started over. Millie discovered she was perfectly capable of drawing little chicken boxes to scale, as long as she didn't have to actually be the boss, the one to decide anything. So she drew, and Sam measured, and Eliza bossed them around and caught their mistakes.

By Friday, there was a plan. A good one. They were all in agreement. Eliza walked up to the whiteboard and wrote their team name—the Egg-ceptionals—under the header READY TO BUILD. And then she did a little pirouette. Sam pumped his fists above his head, and Millie smiled. The Egg-ceptionals were on their way, along with the Egg-celerators and the Eggs-traterrestials. The other groups weren't far behind.

The old Millie would've gone super overboard with the chicken-and-egg jokes herself; even now she felt a few tickle at the edges of her brain like memories, almost—about all the egg-citement, about the intrepid egg-splorers setting their alarm clucks—but instead of turning into more ideas, and better ones, they just sort of floated away before she could utter even a single one out loud. The next thing you know, Reuben and Sam were running with their own comedy routine from one side of the room to the other, only their jokes all seemed to mention whisking and frying, which Millie found zero-percent amusing.

"Not funny," she said, under her breath.

Reuben heard her anyway. "Ooooh, what happened to Millie?" he asked. "I suspect *fowl* play." That got a good laugh from everyone except, well, Millie. How did they not understand that there was a time and a place for kidding around and that this was for sure not it? Lives were at stake!

Teams who were "ready to build" could start on Monday, Ms. Fritz said, but they'd need help. Every team had to have a mentor. Millie's dad used to be the kind of dad who'd do stuff like that—volunteer in science class or chaperone a field trip or whatever. He'd helped Tess with her box when she was in seventh grade. But that was back before he met Silver and moved to an apartment where someone else—a handyman, probably—did every single thing that needed tools or a ladder or a plug. There was no way Dad 2.0 would help with this kind of thing, even if he didn't live so far away. Millie's mom, on the other hand, used tools on a daily basis to fix the smoke alarms and the dishwasher and the bathtub drain, but she was way too busy for brooding boxes. Millie knew better than to even ask.

"My dad's busy with his own class," said Sam, "and this is so not my mom's jam." Sam's mom worked at the same hospital as Millie's mom, but she was a different kind of nurse, the kind who mostly sat a computer all day, with non-brooding-box-ish responsibilities.

"Neither of my parents are all that good at stuff like this either," said Eliza as she shoved her binder into the backpack.

It was starting to seem like the Egg-ceptionals might be one of the teams who were assigned a random PTA volunteer, and let's be real, nobody wanted that. (It would be eggs-cruciating, thought Millie, just for the most fleeting moment.)

Then, instead of making a joke, she said, "I'll ask Tess. Tess has done this whole project before and she's good at stuff like this. Maybe she can help us."

The bell rang right then, and they all pushed through the classroom door into the hall, Sam looking at Millie like she had lost her mind. Tess? Whose favorite activities were mocking Millie, correcting Millie, shaking her head and gnashing her teeth at Millie? That Tess?

Yes. That Tess.

Ugh. What was Millie thinking? Why couldn't she have kept her big mouth shut?

Chapter 14

One weekend a month, Tess and Millie and Lucy went into the city to spend the weekend with Dad and Silver. In the beginning, it had just been Dad—Silver always had to visit her sick mother or go on business trips when the girls came to stay. But that changed, and now it didn't seem like Silver ever had to go anywhere.

If you knew Tad Donally before Silver, you'd never guess he'd ever, in a million years, go for an apartment with white leather couches. Or weirdly shaped mirrors in the kitchen and dining room and bedroom. Or rugs that might've originally been polar bears or weasels or something. Tad Donally had lived with his wife and daughters and dogs in a house with plaid couches and ordinary mirrors above the bathroom sink and on the backs of bedroom doors. Tad Donally used to be the King of Breakfast—that's what he called himself, the Master of Pancakes—but these days, he mostly took the girls out to restaurants when they visited him. For breakfast, lunch, and dinner.

Millie hadn't seen her dad since Lolo, and she didn't really want to. He was going to say something about it, she was positive. He was going to try to make her feel better, but in that too-loud, fake-voice way. Nearly everything her dad did these days was fake. And loud. It wasn't that she didn't miss him—she did, it was just that she also missed him when she was with him. The old, original him.

"This'll be good for you, baby," said Mom to Millie as she put the girls on the train. "To get out of town, to be with your dad for a couple of days. Really. I promise."

Millie knew that wasn't a promise her mom could make, or at least not a promise that she could keep. And so she didn't blame her mom exactly, but she did doubt her.

"M&Ms!" said Lucy, as soon as they'd settled into their seats. "Mom sent M&Ms!" And she handed a bag each to Tess and Millie. Mom never put them on the train to Chicago without a treat. Millie tried not to think of the treats as bribes but she was pretty sure that was what they were. Lucy was supposed to be good and brave and say please and thank you, and Millie was supposed to keep an eye on Lucy and not fight with Tess, and Tess was supposed to call if there was any trouble. And they were all were just expected to go, whether they wanted to or not, whether they were missing a birthday party or a soccer game or a sleepover. Yep. The M&Ms were bribes, for sure. Even if they were yummy. The candy was long gone by the time the girls reached Union Station.

"Why does Silver have to come with Dad to pick us up?" asked Tess. Tess had asked that same question in those same words the month before, and the month before that. Which meant it wasn't really a question. Neither Millie nor Lucy answered.

Lucy flipped the built-in wheels out of the bottoms of her sneakers and rolled off the train and through the turnstile, top speed. "Daddy!" she said.

"Kiddos! Good to see you! Say hi to Silver, everyone."

The girls all kind of mumbled *hi* and then Silver smiled at their dad instead of actually saying *hi* back. Which was pretty standard.

"OK, girls, bright lights, big city," said Dad as they stepped out of the station into the blinking, starry noisiness of Chicago.

But Millie was stuck for a second in the spinny, dizzy glow. She just stood there as everyone went ahead, until suddenly there was Tess with her hand on Millie's shoulder, giving it a soft, quiet, Mom-like squeeze.

"Lolo," whispered Millie, but sort of sadly, because even though she wanted Lolo to be in these lights, too, she knew that she wasn't.

"Lolo?" asked Tess.

"Never mind," said Millie, knowing it wouldn't make any sense to Tess, especially here. These lights were different than the light in the Acostas' window. Louder. Less musical. Less tenderhearted. So Tess just gave her another little pat and then nudged her onto the sidewalk behind Lucy on her wheels and Dad and Silver.

At dinner, Dad brought up Lolo as Millie had expected he would, but he did it in this weird and formal way, more like he was offering condolences to strangers than talking to his own daughters. "Girls, Silver and I want you know how sorry we are about the Acostas' baby."

Silver nodded along as he spoke, and she had tears in her eyes. That was a surprise. Millie didn't know that Silver cried.

"We know it's been really hard for everyone," Dad said.

"It has," said Tess. "It really has." As if it were her story. Her hard thing. As if the *sorry* were just for her.

Millie, meanwhile, just sat there. She didn't cry like Silver or nod along with Dad or agree with Tess. She just sat there. And then the waiter arrived with a tray of those giant, icy sodas in red plastic cups and the topic of conversation moved quickly to other, littler things.

After the restaurant, where everyone had really good, gooey, deep-dish pizza except Silver who had salad because Silver basically had salad at every meal ("Mom would've had pizza," whispered Tess), it was already almost time to go to bed. That was one good thing about weekends in Chicago; they went by quickly.

Once the sleeping arrangements had been negotiated, and Millie—surprise, surprise—was assigned the air mattress yet again (because Tess and Lucy slept best together on the pull-out couch, according to Tess, of course), Dad started acting weird. First he leaned on the doorjamb of the bathroom while Millie brushed her teeth.

"So, kiddo," he said. Millie couldn't answer because her mouth was full of bristles and paste, and that seemed to stump her dad, so he just stood there watching her in a trying-to-be-sweet-but-semi-creepy way.

Then he trailed her when she walked into the kitchen for a glass of water. "How would you say you're doing, Mills?" he asked. And then he tapped out some sort of dad rock-and-roll rhythm on the countertop, which kind of blew the mood but also reminded Millie of the old, King of Breakfast kind of dad he used to be. She smiled and then filled her glass from the fancy dispenser in the fridge and said, "Mmmm, I'm fine," hoping that would be enough. Dad stopped tapping.

"OK, so kiddo," he tried again and followed her back into the living room. She slipped into the plasticky sleeping bag and sank down onto the air mattress. He pulled a shaggy white ottoman over and sat down. Not a good sign.

"Your mom and I were talking," he said, and for one half of a second, Millie's heart leapt. That was a good and human thing—a promising thing—for a mom and a dad to talk, right? ". . . and we think it's really a good idea for you go back to that therapist. Was her name Deena?"

So much for her hopeful, leaping heart. "Um, yes," said Millie. "I mean, no. I mean, yes, her name is Deena, but no, I really, really don't want to go see her again. I already told Mom. I'm fine. I promise!" She fake-smiled to prove it. Her dad did not make dorky drumming noises in response.

"The thing is," he said, "you're not. You're not yourself, Millie. You're kind of hanging back from things, you're kind of quiet. And I get it—this is such a sad, sad thing. But it's time to . . ."

Don't say it, thought Millie. Do not say "get over it." Whatever you do, don't you dare say "get over it."

". . . move on," he said. Which was the same thing.

"Easy for you to say," said Millie.

"What do you mean?" Dad shifted on the shaggy footstool. He sighed. He probably wanted to be back in the bedroom with Silver and the white-noise machine and the automatic window blinds and the scent of the cleaning lady's furniture polish.

And Tess and Lucy, who seemed to be taking a very, very, very long time brushing their teeth, probably wanted to be out here on the pull-out couch with the remote control. They were obviously giving Millie and Dad space—space that Millie didn't want at all.

"What do you mean, 'Easy for you to say'?" Dad repeated.

"You're all about moving on. You don't live near us or come to our performances or even act like our dad anymore," said Millie, and she meant it. He was going to lecture *her* about not being involved? "You're not the Master of Pancakes, you're the Master of Moving On!"

That last bit came out loud and hoarse. Millie had never said anything like it to her dad before. She felt like Tess, strong and mature and opinionated! What a way to end the day. The left-over pizza was in the fancy fridge, the apartment was dark and quiet, and Millie had mic-dropped in a big way. She didn't feel good, exactly, but she felt powerful.

Dad stood up and shook out his pant legs. "See, this is what we mean," he said. "There's stuff to sort out, and the therapist could help with that." He waited for her to answer and when she didn't (because you don't keep talking after a mic drop), he said, "We love you, Mills." And he leaned over and kissed her forehead before heading into bed.

Leaving Millie lying there alone, wondering, Who is *we*?

Chapter 15

Tess was surprised—actually, "shocked"; that's what she said, "I'm shocked"—when Millie asked her if she'd be the Egg-ceptionals' mentor for building their brooding box. Millie felt dumb for asking then, and almost took it back, but before she could, Tess agreed. Millie knew it was because seventh grade science met at the same time as Tess's workout club, and Tess Did Not Like workout club. She said it was just her gym teacher's way of trying to make gym class sound 'cool,' which it definitely wasn't.

Mom sounded kind of shocked about the arrangement, too. "Oh, how nice," she said. "What a nice, nice idea and a great way for you two to spend time together." And then she had to turn her attention to Lucy, who was saying on repeat, "A brooding box? What's a brooding box? What's a brooding box?"

Anyway, in spite of being accused of doing a good deed, Tess really did agree to save the Egg-ceptionals from having to work with a random PTA volunteer, and Millie was grateful. Three times a week for the next two weeks, at 11:15 a.m. (otherwise known as the time for dreaded Workout Club), Tess would walk across the parking lot that separated the middle school from the high school to give Millie and Sam and Eliza her *expertise*. That's what she called it. Eggs-pertise, Millie thought with a little glimmer, but she bit her tongue.

Honestly, Tess was being almost nice to Millie these days— ever since that meltdown in the living room a couple of weeks earlier when Millie'd become a whirling dervish of wild rage, and Tess had barely escaped intact. Ever since, she'd given Millie more space than usual but also, somehow, she had been a little sweeter and gotten a little closer. If that made sense.

Even standing together over the brooding box schematics in Ms. Fritz's room, there was this . . . feeling. This sense that Tess was there for her, that she had Millie's back. This was not a feeling that Millie was used to, but she kind of liked it.

But here's what she hadn't accounted for: Since their official team mentor was her own personal big sister, Millie was thrust back into the limelight, just when she was getting really good at letting Sam and Eliza basically run the show. With Tess on board, everyone's favorite question suddenly seemed to be "OK, yeah. And what do you think, Millie?"

Had her own standing increased simply because she'd arranged to have a high schooler help them out? Millie wasn't sure, but it was not her favorite thing. She wished, instead, that they'd look at Tess as her stand-in, and leave her out of the decision-making altogether. But no.

"What do you think about reinforcing the corners, Millie?"

"What do you think about using a metal screen here, Millie?"

"Millie, what do you think about moving the clips for the lamps up, like this?"

Each time Millie just wanted to answer, "Warmth and light, warmth and light, warmth and light," like a song but not even with real words, more like the hum she seemed to live in these days, the hum that came with Lolo's light. But Millie wasn't a fool. She knew if she responded to questions with some weird, airy, bioluminescent hum, eyes would be rolled, calls would be made, and she'd be driven directly from school to Deena the Family Therapist.

So instead, she practiced saying things like "Yes" and "Sounds good" and nodding her head and blinking through her wire-rimmed glasses, which worked kind of like a shield she could hide herself behind. She nodded and blinked and said anything she could muster to show that she was present. Normal. Chiming in but not in charge. And Tess and Sam and Eliza practiced nodding back and saying things like "OK, great," like everything was totally fine, like nothing was off or awkward with the Egg-ceptionals at all.

It was really only Tess who, sometimes, quietly, would say, "Mills . . . ?" like even her name had become something impossible to figure out.

Millie would swallow all the words in the dictionary except *yep*, and she'd say that one super casual, like she didn't hear the worry in Tess's voice. Somehow that was enough to keep her sister at bay a little longer.

Each class period, amid all the noise and action, the adjusted plans and disagreements and construction—made even noisier by all the extra people in the room—a couple of moms and dads, a grandfather, and, yes, a dreaded PTA volunteer—Ms. Fritz would pull a few kids away from their building project to go to the big walk-in coolers where the eggs were being stored, to turn them. On certain days, inevitably, Millie had to go.

"One rep from each team again today," Ms. Fritz would say, and then she'd point at Millie and Aisha and Nicholas and Reuben and a few others, and send them—on their own—to the eggs. *On their own*, to just nonchalantly twist the eggs about, as if they were turning on a faucet or opening a jar of spaghetti sauce or something. As if it were nothing!

When it was her turn, Millie took each cool, smooth egg in her right hand and stared at one invisible but crucial spot on the shell while she turned it, slowly, clockwise, until that one spot had moved just out of sight. Even then, she wondered if she'd done it quite right. If the egg—if the tiny possibility *inside* the egg—would be OK.

Meanwhile, as Millie was off turning the eggs, Sam and Eliza and Tess were on *their* own with the brooding box. That's how Millie thought of them—on their own—even though she was relieved to be away from the ongoing second-guessing and interrogation for a few minutes, and even though Tess, technically, knew what she was doing. When she got back from the coolers, Millie looked everything over very carefully, in case the project had been sabotaged in some way. She didn't say out loud how worried she was, but she was indeed very worried.

In spite of all this worry and weirdness, the Egg-ceptionals' brooding box was born. Tess, it turns out, was kind of a master builder. Like, you should have seen her with the finishing nails and carpenter's square, making everything plumb and tight. (These were carpentry words Tess threw around without a thought. "There we go," she'd say, "perfectly plumb.") Millie didn't want to make a big deal about it, but she was impressed; Tess was an expert after all. And Eliza's perfectionist streak had paid off, too. Even Sam had to admit that plywood was better than cardboard in the end.

The box would do what it needed to do—provide warmth and light, warmth and light, warmth and light. It ran through Millie's head like a recording. But she could see that this was actually more than just that. Way more. Together they'd built a beautiful box—if brooding boxes could be beautiful. They'd finished it and double checked it and taken pictures of it. And then they'd set it firmly in place on the counter that ran along the back wall of the science room, which was where it would become an incubator for the refrigerated eggs.

"Let the Egg-ceptionals," announced Sam now, in a sort of boomy, circus-barker voice that echoed across the room, "serve as eggs-amples to the rest of you!" And then he said, more softly, "Come on you guys, bow!"

Eliza and Sam swept into deep, dramatic bows in front of their box, while Millie tilted forward just slightly, one eye still on the box. The kids standing around them laughed and clapped slow, sarcastic, seventh-grade claps.

Tess stood just off to the side, which was unusual for her. Millie glanced over, trying to figure out what was going on, and could see, clear as day, that Tess was as proud as the rest of the team, but quietly. Thank you, Millie thought. Thank you, Tess. And she hoped with all her might that Tess could read her mind.

"OK, OK, you self-proclaimed superheroes. This is all good stuff, but you're not done," said Ms. Fritz. She was kind of laughing, but you could tell she meant business. "Remember that your eggs are going to need to be kept as close to 99.5 degrees Fahrenheit as possible at all times. The boxes I'm seeing so far are looking good, but starting Monday, let's take a few days to watch our temperature and humidity values very carefully. It's time to refine all the parameters."

"Oh, bummer," said Eliza and Sam.

"OK, phew," said Millie, at the exact same time.

They gave her a funny look, totally not getting her utter relief at being given another chance to double-triple-quadruple-check everything. But then they just said "jinx" to each other as if Millie hadn't spoken at all. Even though jinx is something that would usually happen between her and Sam.

The Egg-ceptionals did not technically need Tess for this part of their project, for the switching on the lab lamps and setting up the thermistor and generally making sure that all the conditions would be just right for those eggs that were still stowed in the walk-in cooler behind the cafeteria line. Tess had helped them make the perfect brooding box—that was her job, and she was done with that. They all were.

"But, I was thinking," she said as they were all packing up their stuff at the end of class, "I could still come for a few more days. Like, just to make sure about everything, right?" The Egg-ceptionals agreed. Why not?

"Plus, then I get to skip Workout Club with Missy Lowell, and you know how I feel about Workout Club and Missy Lowell." Millie did know.

So Tess just kept coming, and honestly, it seemed like she liked it. She and Sam and Eliza played with the lamps—raising and lowering the clips so that the brooding box got too cool and then too warm—and they added the straw bedding and they prepped the screen top. They were turning their brooding box into a proper incubator. Millie, meanwhile, took pictures and measurements and notes. She looked over their shoulders and made sure they were doing and testing and recording everything exactly right.

Mostly, though, she worried. She was beginning to think of worrying as her official job.

One day, when Millie said, "OK, so you guys, I'm concerned…," Eliza tried to shut her down by saying, "For someone who didn't want to be in charge, you sure do want to be in charge."

Millie was not dissuaded.

"No, stop!" she called out more than once during their trials. "It's getting too hot. Stop!" She reached over and clicked off one of the heat lamps.

"That's not your job, to turn off the lights!" said Eliza. "That's the thermistor's job! You have to let the machine do it. That's how we'll know it's working!"

"Someone's getting hot and bothered over there in Egg-ceptional Land," said Reuben. As if it were even slightly his business.

"Might need to take a chill pill, Mill," said Nicholas, who was suddenly a poet.

Millie's cheeks flushed—she really was hot and bothered—and she looked at Sam, thinking he was going to defend her the way he had on other days when Eliza'd gotten kind of testy with her, but he didn't. For maybe the first time in her whole long life, he didn't. He just said, "There aren't any eggs in there yet, Millie." He sounded tired. He sounded tender but also really tired.

Plus, he seemed to have complete faith in the auto-on, auto-off capacity of a little tiny circuit that was supposed to keep the light bulbs from frying the eggs. And the opposite—he trusted that the circuit would keep the lights *on* long enough to make sure the growing embryos stayed alive inside their inscrutable shells. Ms. Fritz must have had faith, too since she was the one who, by the end of class on Tuesday, approved their plan, and agreed that they were ready, really ready now, for their eggs.

Warmth and light, warmth and light, warmth and light, thought Millie, as if that was all they had to worry about. But why was nothing ever as simple as it seemed?

Chapter 16

When Millie came downstairs for breakfast, she could hear her mom and Tess talking in the kitchen, which was weird, since Millie usually beat Tess down. Tess's trademark move was to fly down the steps at the very last possible second, just in time to grab a piece of peanut butter toast as she ran out the door with her ponytail flying behind her like a flag.

So the fact that they were in there together, talking, was weird enough that Millie paused—her left foot still resting on the last step, her breath held—to try to figure out what was going on.

". . . it's like she's not a real kid, Mom. Like, she's there in the room with us . . . I mean, even with Sam of all people! She likes him more than she likes any of us, right? But she doesn't really talk to him anymore. Like, at all. She's become like a ghost or a robot or something. A super-tense, scary, angry ghost or robot."

Millie's foot dropped from the stair with a slow thump. She set her backpack down and then she sat down, too, right there on the floor, amid the dog hair and leashes and umbrellas and shoes. She wrapped her arms around her body and thought, I don't feel like a ghost or a robot. I feel like a real kid. Aren't I a real kid?

The thing about Tess, even though she could be a little bit of a braggy show-off, was that she was usually right about everything. Maybe all big sisters were almost always right— Millie didn't know because Tess was her only test case. But either way, if Tess said Millie wasn't real, maybe she wasn't. Millie felt her hair and jeans and the skin of her arms underneath her sweatshirt. It bristled, goosebumpy, like real skin, but when she bit down on her lip it didn't bleed or even hurt. It tasted a little bit like metal.

"Oh, Tess. All of this is so sad." Meg Donally let out the sort of exhausted, noisy exhale she usually reserved for after work. "This is just what I was afraid of. I don't know. . . . I don't . . ."

They were all just completely quiet for a minute then—Tess and Mom, and also Millie, her lip still tightly held between her teeth, waiting to see what Mom was going to say.

"Well, anyway, honey . . . thank you. Thank you for keeping an eye on her. Thank you for loving her."

"OK. Sorry, Mom," said Tess, with not an ounce of snark.

"I know, sweets. We're all just doing our best here. But grief is a tremendous thing. I . . . I seem to need some help, and so does Millie. . . ."

Millie imagined them hugging then. That's what Mom did at the end of hard conversations like this. And as Mom and Tess hugged, Millie thought, Tess has been secretly spying on me. When she was supposed to be helping build and measure and test and ensure the just-rightness of the brooding box, she'd actually been spying.

Or, babysitting.

Right then, before Millie had a chance to get really mad, there was a crash. "Oh, fudge!" Millie's mom said. "Ugh—all over my scrubs." And before Millie could breathe or budge, her mom appeared in front of her, coffee splattered all along one leg, and her mouth open in a long, sad oval.

"Oh, Millie. Oh, hi, baby. This morning is really . . . I just . . ." She leaned over to give Millie a one-armed hug and then, instead of stopping and saying something clear and helpful like she would usually do, she kept moving right past Millie and headed up the stairs.

In the kitchen, Tess was sort of half-heartedly sweeping up the broken mug as the dogs licked the milky coffee off the floor.

"The dogs shouldn't be in here," said Millie. "They're going to cut their feet or their tongues or something."

"Oh," said Tess. "Good point." Which was a weird thing for the always-right girl to say to the un-real robot girl, but then she didn't actually do anything about it—she just kind of stood there with the broom in her hands and let the dogs keep licking up the coffee. Millie pushed all the dogs out the back door and grabbed some paper towels to help. But then the toast popped up and Tess handed her the broom and said, "I gotta go. I'm gonna see if I can get a ride early from Nathan. I've got . . ."

She trailed off because she didn't have a reason. She didn't need a ride, she didn't need to get to school early. She just needed to get away from Millie, and Millie knew it.

"Um, OK," said Millie, popping her own toast down, knowing that her mom wouldn't have even a second now to do anything but change, rush Lucy into her clothes, and fly out the door to work. Not even a second to reassure Millie. To tell her that she knew, deep down, that everything would be OK. Millie was on her own, with the dogs and the toast, and she'd be on her own for the walk to school. Usually she didn't mind that. On alone days she could linger just a little as she passed the Acostas', she'd pause just out of sight, on the other side of the street, and say hello to Lolo's light before walking the rest of the way in the peaceful quiet. But today, after hearing all that . . .

"Millie," called her mom from halfway down the stairs, "can you buy lunch today, sweets? I'm out of time and Lucy's dawdling. And could you quickly feed the dogs?" As if things really were OK, as if *she* were OK. Just normal old Millie.

She scooped kibble into the dogs' bowls and rubbed the sticker off an apple from the fruit drawer in the fridge. She didn't like hot lunch. She never had, but especially now, because hot lunch meant more time in the cafeteria with, well, everyone. What Millie liked to do instead was go into Ms. Fritz's room over lunch. She liked to inspect their brooding box and recalculate various measurements—out of earshot of Tess and Sam and Eliza. She liked to make sure the light and the thermistor hadn't shifted. She liked to double-check that everything for those budding baby chicks was just so. Actually, maybe *liked* was a little bit of an exaggeration. It's just what she felt she *should* do.

Sometimes Ms. Fritz chatted with Millie or asked her for help with something or other in the classroom, and sometimes she just let her be. Millie liked Ms. Fritz, so she was fine either way. Today, as Millie sat down near the back of the room, took her apple from her bag, and looked over all the brooding boxes, she thought, Shouldn't a proper incubator have a cover?

Ms. Fritz came up behind her. Sat down. Stared at the incubators with Millie. And then, after a while, said, "Don't take this the wrong way, Millie, but is everything OK? I mean, you've been coming in here during lunch a lot lately and . . . wouldn't you rather be with your friends?"

"I'm worried," said Millie. She didn't know what made her say that. It just popped out. Her apple sat heavy in the palm of her hand. Millie studied it. Wished it were more interesting or complicated. Wished it required something of her, offered her something distracting to do.

"You're worried?" said Ms. Fritz. "About what?"

"Shouldn't a real incubator have a cover?" Millie said, looking up from the apple, knowing that a cover wasn't even the half of it.

Ms. Fritz laughed, then, but not in a mean way. "Millie, your box is spectacular. What do you say we move the eggs in tomorrow? Worry is always the worst before something happens, right? Once the eggs are in the boxes, everything's going to be fine. The experiment will just unfold!"

Even though Millie liked Ms. Fritz, she knew this wasn't true. Worry is not the worst before something happens. Most things—the darkest, hardest things—happen before you even know to worry about them. Millie knew this, and she wondered how on earth a grown-up could have survived this long without knowing it, too.

"Do Mr. Clark's groups all have covers on their boxes?" Sam always said his dad was the stricter teacher, and Millie was starting to think that strict wouldn't be such a bad thing. Maybe she should've asked to be in his class. Maybe more eggs make it through in there.

"I've been doing this a long time, Millie," said Ms. Fritz. "There's no one right way to build a brooding box, I assure you. Just so long as you can keep the eggs warm."

"That's what I've been saying!" said Millie. "Warmth and light!"

"Yes," said Ms. Fritz. "Well, that's good. We agree, then. And tomorrow—the eggs! Yes?" And then she went back to eat lunch at her desk, leaving Millie to keep worrying on her own.

On her way home that day, Millie paused across from the Acostas', just like she had that morning. And there was Lolo's light, beaming even more brightly than usual. It felt like the whole house was light now—light and yellow and warm and beating like a heart, which almost made her say, "Lolo?" but instead she said, "Are you even real? Am I making you up?"

When there was no answer, Millie felt a hollowness at her center, and all of a sudden, the light was not enough. Even this huge, warm, pulsing sun of a house was not enough to fill her up, to warm her or comfort her or show her the way. She wanted more. She thought what she'd wanted was for everyone—Ms. Fritz and Sam and Eliza . . . Mom and Tess . . . even Dad—to understand her, to agree with her, to worry with her.

But that wasn't really it, and she knew that now. What Millie wanted was to be OK. She felt it in her bones. She wanted to be OK. She wanted her incubator and eggs to be OK. She wanted the Acostas to be OK, and she wanted little Lolo to be OK, too.

"Oh, Lolo," she said, quietly and a little less sure, even, than before.

But instead of Lolo, Mr. Acosta appeared like magic, right across the street. He was looking straight at her—he was actually waving at her. Millie's face flushed. She looked farther up the street toward her house, as if she might make a break for it because She. Did. Not. Want. This. Whatever this was. She wasn't ready to just bump into Mr. Acosta on her way home from school. She wasn't ready at all. But her feet stayed anchored where they were—they seemed to know there was no escape.

Millie didn't know if Mr. Acosta had come from the house or the garage or the side yard, but it didn't matter because there he stood with a big, brown cardboard box in his arms and a golden glow around his head, like a crown, like those paintings at the Art Institute they'd seen on their field trip last year. She hadn't seen the Acostas since that day in the church with the tiny casket and the giant, broken Jesus, and all at once she wondered where they'd been all this time. Did they not pick up their mail anymore? Did they not take out their garbage or water their plants? Did they not go to work?

Her mind raced like this until Mr. Acosta, standing in the house's buzzy glow, called from across the street. "Millie?" he said. "Hey, Millie."

"Hey," said Millie, and then she shivered.

Mr. Acosta stepped off the curb toward her, and so she stepped toward him, too, not because she wanted to, but because she was being pulled by that familiar, nearly invisible sheen of light.

"We've been meaning to come and see you again, Millie. We've . . . Katherine and I, we've wanted to know how you were doing. Like, how is school for you and everything? But we just haven't . . . well . . . anyway, here you are."

Millie squinted as she got closer to the Acostas' house—the light growing brighter and brighter, pulsing—until Mr. Acosta was almost just an outline in front of it. It was real, she thought. This is the realest light in the world.

"Yep," she said. "Here I am." And that's when she realized she should've visited *them*. Instead of just walking by and staring through their windows every day, she should've stopped and rang the bell, told them she was thinking about them, asked if they needed anything. She should've made them cookies or banana bread. Why hadn't she? It was as if she'd been blinded by the light without realizing it.

"Right. OK. Well, how are you?" asked Mr. Acosta. "Are you OK? Are you getting by?"

Millie didn't know how to answer that. Was she getting by? All her friends were avoiding her and her own sister thought she was a robot. Was she supposed to tell Mr. Acosta *that*? Was she supposed to say that she slept curled tightly with her dogs in the glow of a night-light now, like she had when she was a little girl? That she stumbled from school to sleep, and back again? That she spent her lunch period hiding out in the dim, gaping space of a science room, making small talk with a teacher? Did Mr. Acosta really need to know any of that?

Millie pictured herself as one of the eggs they'd be moving into the incubators tomorrow—you couldn't tell by looking at her what was going on inside. She was just a shell of herself, and inside she might be whole and healthy, she might be broken or hollow or achy or gone. She thought she should stay like that—hidden inside her own shell. She was safer that way. At least with Mr. Acosta. At least for now.

"Um, I'm . . . OK," said Millie. "How . . . how are you?" Millie knew it was a dumb question—or at least too small a question—but it was just what you asked after somebody asked you. Millie wished that this had been one of her mom's lessons—along with the ones about SIDS and funerals and condolence cards. How to talk to the Acostas. How to not say dumb things. How to let them know that she really understood how much they loved Lolo and that in some very true way, she did, too.

"Aw, thanks, Millie," said Mr. Acosta. "Y'know. We're hanging in there. We are moving through our days."

Millie nodded. She didn't know that could be an answer—that you could just be moving through your days and say so. She also didn't know that a man could be suspended in light, just floating there like a bug in amber, and not notice it or say something.

"Do you know about bioluminescence?" asked Millie. She knew she shouldn't be talking about chicks or incubators or thermistors to Mr. Acosta, but bioluminescence . . . that seemed different and somehow related to their conversation. "Like, how certain things make light? Or are light? Well, actually, both, kind of?"

Mr. Acosta shifted the box from one hip to another and the light swirled around him as he did. "Um, yes. Bioluminescence. Yeah, I think I remember learning about that. It's like glowworms and certain fish and such. Right?"

Millie and Mr. Acosta were standing right in the middle of the street now, right next to each other, awash in the very bioluminescent buzz from the house behind him. Millie looked up into Mr. Acosta's eyes and said, "Yes. But really, it's everywhere, once you start looking for it. It's all over the place." And she made a big circle with her arms, a big sweeping circle that drew

Mr. Acosta and his cardboard box and the trash cans on the curb and even herself and her backpack into Lolo's light.

"OK," said Mr. Acosta. "OK, so I'll look for it, then." And he smiled at Millie. Like he was grateful. Like she had given him a gift.

You don't need to look for it, she wanted to say. It's all around you! Here it is!

But instead she said, "OK. Well, I gotta go." And before Mr. Acosta could answer, that's just what Millie did.

Chapter 17

Sam was one of the boys whose voice hadn't changed yet. He had the voice he'd always had, for as long as Millie could remember. If she wanted to, she could stand in the middle of a crowded corridor that ran straight down the middle of a crowded school and hear that voice and *know* it was Sam—the same Sam she'd known forever, the same Sam who'd always known her.

The truth is, *everyone* knew that voice, because Sam was a little bit of a class clown. Sometimes a teacher would hush him by putting a finger up to pursed lips, or by saying, "All right, pipe down, Mr. Clark, pipe down." Nobody ever actually got mad at him—including Millie—maybe because his dad was a teacher, so he had a get-out-of-jail-free card, or maybe because he really was only joking around.

Lately, Millie was just grateful when Sam talked so she didn't have to, no matter the topic. But when Ms. Fritz, on egg day, said, "OK, quiet down for this next step, gang. Let's carefully and quietly move these eggs into their incubators. Let's stay completely focused," Sam didn't quiet down or focus. He went back to punning.

"You mean eggs-actly focused, Ms. Fritz?" Everyone laughed except Millie. Even Ms. Fritz was sort of laughing as she shook her head.

Somehow all the laughter pushed Sam to go further—like he was performing and the attention made him forget for a second that she wasn't the old Millie, the funny, easy one he used to know. He said, "What's the matter, Mills? Can't you take a *yolk*? Don't I *crack* you up? Eggs-cuse . . ."

And Millie, before she was even able to think the words to herself, wheeled around and said through clenched teeth, "No. You don't. You don't crack me up and it's not funny and I can't take a joke! Shut up, Sam!"

Sam shut up. So did everyone else. Millie's face burned, but she didn't take it back. She didn't say sorry, because she wasn't. She meant it. She wanted perfect silence. She wanted everyone to move softly and slowly, into the walk-in cooler and then back to class, holding the eggs out in front of them like a tray of something fragile—crystal goblets, maybe, or light bulbs. Or—duh—eggs. Yes, fragile, like the eggs they were! Why weren't people taking this seriously? Why wasn't Sam?

"OK, OK, everyone. No worries. All's well," said Ms. Fritz. "This is careful work, but exciting! Let's enjoy this next phase of the project."

And Millie, who was genuinely mad now, thought, You lost me at "enjoy."

Each group was going to get six eggs. Eliza carried a great big container of twenty-four into the classroom, and Tristan carried the other twenty-four. Millie tiptoed along next to them as they moved through the room, even though she wasn't technically one of the transporters.

"Remember," Ms. Fritz said, "that when you shift your eggs into your brooding boxes, you'll want to turn them because they've been in this position for a little over twenty-four hours now, right?"

Turning an egg is different than putting a math test either faceup or facedown on a desk because, with an egg, where does one side end and the other begin? This had worried Millie when she'd been one of the ones sent to turn the eggs, and it worried her still. And what about kids like Nicholas—who'd gone with her one day last week—who didn't care about anything, not school or brushing his hair or eggs. What if the Egg-ceptionals got the eggs Nicholas had turned? Then what? (Deep down, Millie understood that *someone* would get those eggs, but all she could manage to think about right now—all she could hope for— were the six that would land in her particularly egg-ceptional brooding box.)

"Oh, and also . . . ," said Ms. Fritz, as if she was just randomly thinking of instructions as she went along—as if it didn't matter what order the instructions came in or whether she gave them at all—

Millie butted in—"We'll want to double-check that each box is still the same temperature!"—a little louder and more desperate-sounding than she'd planned. (Now she was the loud one!)

"OK, right," said Ms. Fritz. "I don't think that's exactly what I was going to say but OK, yes. Good point, Millie." Sam stepped farther away from Millie and turned his back to her so she couldn't see his face at all. Millie didn't like thinking of him as a stranger, but right now she felt totally and completely alone.

And then, even though Ms. Fritz wasn't exactly done talking, Tristan and Eliza started distributing eggs. They began on opposite sides of the room, ready to stop at various plastic, plywood, simple, fancy, clunky, and futuristic brooding boxes to make the transfer of eggs. It would take a while, and everyone clumped around, laughing and fist-bumping and generally risking the lives of a lot of little chicks. Were they seventh-grade sociopaths, or what? But all the chaos meant that Millie had a minute to double-check their box one last time—not just the temperature and humidity, but the seal at the corners, the soft bed of hay, the labels. Everything.

She did this on her own, since Eliza was handing out eggs, and Sam . . . well, Sam had moved over to the other side of the room. She could hear him drumming his fingers on the metal radiator underneath the windows. Apparently not looking at her wasn't enough—he needed to actually get physically away from her and drum with an angry sort of thunder as a way of saying, *I won't shut up, I won't be more careful, and you can't make me.*

Millie felt, at her center, right where her lungs touched her belly, a kind of burning ache. She knew it was there because of Sam and what she'd said to him and how he'd taken it and turned it into this terrible finger drumming, but she didn't care. She couldn't get distracted. She just kept her head down and examined every little aspect of their box. Somebody had to.

When she finally looked up, she realized that the Egg-ceptionals, stuck about halfway down the counter in the middle of everything, were going to get the last six eggs from Eliza's tray. Eggs that might've been left for last for a reason. They might've been roughed up. They could already be sick or broken or too warm or too cold, before Millie and Sam and Eliza even had a chance to try to bring them to life.

Time slowed. Millie watched as small, cold eggs were lifted, two-handed, into the other incubators. She watched as her classmates celebrated after settling their eggs into soft straw, how they stepped back and smiled, like that was it, like the whole thing was over already. Achievement unlocked. Riley even said, out loud, "There. We got this. Piece of cake." Millie watched it all with a growing dread.

And then, at last, Eliza arrived next to Millie with her nearly empty tray, light and uneven with just the final six eggs left. Their eggs.

"OK, guys," she said. "Ready?"

Sam appeared next to her and nodded.

"Yes," agreed Millie, but that was a lie. This was not a piece of cake. It was six small and fragile eggs being dropped into a homemade brooding box. Six small and fragile eggs in a homemade brooding box made by a bunch of middle schoolers who were somehow, impossibly, illogically, in charge of keeping them alive. She was most definitely not ready.

Chapter 18

It turns out that making a visit to Deena the Family Therapist is not optional once you've been pegged as a robot girl by your sister the spy. It was like a Forced Family Outing, except Millie was the only one being forced, so it was more like a Mandatory Millie Outing. Her mom didn't even tell her about it until the afternoon of the appointment.

"You didn't bother to ask?" said Millie. "I thought you were on my team."

"I am on your team, baby. Always," said Mom. "I was just thinking Deena could be on the team, too."

If Millie still made jokes she would've made one then, about Deena dropping the ball or fouling out or something. She'd originally been hired to help Millie and her sisters understand divorce. More specifically, their parents' divorce. More specifically, Silver. The problem was, none of that stopped them from missing their dad, or helped them like Silver. Which meant Deena the Family Therapist wasn't wildly successful at her job.

This is what Millie was thinking as she sat in the waiting room with the water dispenser that made that huge, kind of awkward-sounding *bloop* anytime anyone used it. She thought about Deena not being good at her job and she thought about the bubble racing up to the top of the water dispenser—*bloop!*—and she thought about what temperature it better be in the chickens' brooding box right that very second.

She could've just kept thinking and thinking, but then Deena appeared and interrupted her.

"Millie," Deena said, "I'm so glad to see you again." She was wearing a too-tight suit jacket and her skirt was twisted so you could see the zipper. And she was smiling. There might have been lipstick on her teeth, but Millie wasn't going to point that out. Tess probably would have. Tess liked to say things like "Not that I'm the doyenne of fashion, but . . ." and then follow it with a harsh criticism of what you were wearing, doing, or looking like. But Tess wasn't here. Millie was on her own.

Millie's mom reached over and squeezed Millie's hand and then, when she realized Millie wasn't going to speak up—about the lipstick or anything else—she said, "OK, well, thank you, Deena, for fitting us in. Would you like me to come back with you two, or . . ."

Deena kept lipstick-smiling at them, like they were at a birthday party—like she was a hostess instead of a therapist—and said, "Oh, I think we'll be fine on our own, don't you, Millie?"

Millie looked at her mom and thought she saw a glimmer of relief slip over her face like a shadow—just that quickly—like she wasn't even sure it was there.

"OK," said Millie, and she stood up to follow Deena down the hall to her office, leaving her mom behind in the waiting room. Right before Deena shut the office door, Millie heard the water dispenser go *bloop*.

"Well, Millie, before we get started, I just have to say, I really like your new glasses. I didn't even know you wore glasses!" Deena the Family Therapist sat in an armchair with her legs crossed, and Millie sat on the couch across from her.

I know, I didn't, Millie thought. I didn't used to wear glasses. I wore contacts. Until . . . Lolo. Those first few days, after crying a bunch, Millie couldn't seem to get her contacts back in and then, after a while, she didn't really want to. She preferred seeing the world from behind these lenses and she trusted them, resting heavily on the bridge of her nose, to remind her to look, notice, be careful.

But Millie didn't say that. She said, "Thank you." And that's pretty much how the whole rest of the appointment went— Millie thinking one thing and saying something else entirely.

Deena: So, I understand you've been going through a very hard time lately.

Millie's thoughts: When a baby is gone but also some-how weirdly not gone, at least in your head, that's not called a *hard time.* A hard time is when you have a math teacher who isn't very good at explaining fractions. This is different. This is panic. Sorrow. Nearly impossible guilt. And then a tiny sliver of hope before the panic and sorrow and guilt come back again. Back and forth. Over and over. Like a light bulb that's not screwed in right, blinking on and off.

Millie's words: Um, yeah.

Deena: I'm so sorry, Millie.

Millie's thoughts: Why do people keep saying that, that they're sorry? When really *I'm* the one who's sorry. Only, I don't know who to say it to, or even exactly what I'm sorry for, except that I was in charge. I was in charge of keeping Lolo safe.

Millie's words: Thank you.

Deena: Your mom was telling me that they're concerned— she and your dad—about whether or not you're talking to anyone, whether or not you're really processing all this. And basically, whether you're grieving, which is so critically important to moving on. She thought maybe you could do a little of that here, with me.

Millie's thoughts: No way. Not going to happen. Not that I'm the doyenne of fashion or anything, but that lipstick! Also, don't say "moving on."

Millie's words: Um, OK.

Which Deena the Family Therapist understandably took as agreement. She just charged ahead, reminding Millie where the tissues were, and also that she should feel free to pick up or play with anything on the table—the sand garden or the modeling clay or the worry stones.

Deena: Really. Anything. I want you to feel comfortable.

Millie's thoughts: Well, I don't. I feel uncomfortable. I hate being here in this office with the big bloopy water dispenser and the tissues and the awkwardness. And I don't want to talk about Lolo any more than I ever wanted to talk about Silver, which was exactly zero wants.

Millie's words: OK.

And then she reached for the modeling clay. She sat there for thirty-nine more minutes, thinking everything and saying nothing, rubbing and rolling and pinching and squeezing the clay.

Deena: OK, this was a start. It's hard, Millie. We're going to go slowly and carefully, OK? But I'm afraid that we're out of time for today.

Millie's thoughts: Thank dog!

Millie's words: OK. Um, here's a chicken.

And she set a perfectly formed little clay chicken on Deena's table before heading back to her mom, who sat waiting in the lobby with the magazines and two other sad families and the water dispenser. *Bloop.*

Chapter 19

It takes twenty-one days for a chick to hatch once the egg is warming underneath a hen or in an incubator. Twenty-one long, careful, nerve-wracking days. Twenty-one days to go from tiny blastoderm to yolk sac and allantois to egg tooth—to wet, feathery, hatched, alive chick. Twenty-one desperate, uncomfortable, nearly impossible days.

"That's nothing!" said Millie's mom over breakfast. "Compared to a human mom like me . . . I was pregnant for, what, over eight hundred days with the three of you girls?"

"Can I have more brown sugar?" said Lucy, who'd eaten the first melty-sweet top right off her bowl of oatmeal.

"Eight hundred days and everyone *still* needs me!" said Mom, hopping up to get the sugar. She laughed a little in her tired-mom way.

Millie kind of couldn't believe the eight hundred days—that's a ridiculously long amount of time to be pregnant! But her focus was on the twenty-one chicken days that lay dangerously ahead of her. She gobbled down the rest of her breakfast, and by then Tess had come downstairs, too, so they headed off together, toward school, where those eggs were waiting.

"Millie," said Tess, as the front door shut behind them and they started down the sidewalk. "Not that you owe me for helping with your incubator or anything, but . . ."

Millie knew she should listen—and do whatever Tess asked of her—because she actually *did* owe Tess. Their box was the best in the whole class because of her. Plus, maybe if Millie listened, if she played her part in a semi-normal conversation for once, Tess would go back to thinking of her as real instead of robotic and she could wiggle her way out of sessions with Deena. So she tried, she leaned in, even, but Tess's words—about some whole thing with Missy and Rachel, and how Millie could help by maybe getting some scoop from Rachel's little sister—got lost in the waves of light coming from the Acostas', the humming energy that was maybe less promising than it had been a few weeks ago but still, also, somehow, Lolo.

"Does that sound almost like an airplane?" asked Millie.

"Um, what?" said Tess. "Does what sound almost like an airplane?"

They were directly across from the Acostas' now, and the hum had grown into an actual roar in Millie's head.

"The light?" said Millie. She said it like a question. She felt embarrassed, like she hadn't meant to say it out loud.

Tess stopped. She looked at Millie, and then at the Acostas', and then back at Millie. "No, Millie," she said. "It doesn't sound anything like an airplane. You're making things up in your head and it's not helping anything." And then she sighed and kept on walking. Millie did not keep walking. She stood there, head throbbing, nearly blinded from looking straight into the bioluminescent glow that only she could see or hear.

And then she shook her head and ran a little to catch up, but Tess had slipped earbuds in and was singing to herself. As if they hadn't been in the middle of a dramatic, friend-group conversation. As if all that mattered was Ariana Grande or whatever. As if there was no light, no hum, no Lolo. And the farther they walked, the darker it got, and the less Millie believed in any of it either.

Millie used to like school but these days she was just in a hurry to get through it, the first half of the day at least, so she could be with her eggs. Somehow all that yearning made the other classes last even longer. "There ain't no bad joke like a dad joke," said Mr. Brustein, just as the bell rang. Millie had been spacing out and missed the actual joke, but from the groans, she was pretty sure she hadn't missed much.

"OK, OK, thanks for the support," said Mr. Brustein. "Now, get outta here. Go have a great day."

Millie was the first one out the door, as usual. Honestly, she was getting a little faster every day. She was the first one to find her seat in math class. The first one to grab her lunch out of her locker. The first one, always, to Ms. Fritz's room. Was she just imagining that Ms. Fritz sighed when Millie appeared at the door, craning to get a look at the incubators lined up along the back wall, as if just laying her eyes on them made them safer? Was she just imagining that nearly everyone she came in contact with these days sighed when they saw her?

"So, a reminder that a hen," said Ms. Fritz, "would be turning her eggs many times a day—using her beak, using her feet, using her own chicken wisdom and intuition—to make sure everything was just right for her growing chicks, temperature- and humidity-wise." She clicked the clicker and a new slide popped up, of a big, fat, happy-looking hen standing over her eggs.

"But we are not hens," said Ms. Fritz. "We are . . ."

"Babysitters!" shouted Nicholas. A bunch of people who were not Millie laughed.

"Well, I was looking for the word *surrogates*, but OK," Ms. Fritz said. "And it's our responsibility to do just as good a job as this hen might do—keeping the eggs warm, ventilated, and safe. Bringing as many of them to hatching as possible."

"You mean all of them," said Millie, but she said it quietly since things had ended up kind of badly in here yesterday, at least with Sam, and she didn't want to draw any more attention to herself than she already had. She did, however, want every single, solitary egg to hatch. Obviously.

"Well, no. Not *all*," said Ms. Fritz, who'd apparently heard her. "As I've mentioned before, it would be highly unusual for all the eggs to be fertile and grow successfully through the whole incubation period. Right?" She nodded, agreeing with herself. And then she went on.

"Now, today we're going to go over the continued turning and candling, both of which are going to be important steps to take—alongside continually monitoring the climate of our boxes, which we've already talked about and practiced thoroughly."

Millie pulled out her notebook and her pen. Sam didn't. Eliza didn't. How were they supposed to live up to their Egg-ceptionality if they didn't try harder? If they didn't care?

Millie tried to get Sam's attention, to tell him—with her eyes—that he had to take notes and remember every little detail so she wouldn't be alone in keeping these chicks alive. But Sam would not look at her. He had not been waiting for her that morning by the front steps at school. He didn't come by or call last night. Millie didn't know that someone as loud and funny as Sam could even give the silent treatment, but it was pretty obvious that that's what she was getting. Still, she stared and stared at him, hoping, her eyes trained on his profile like magnets. He had to feel them, didn't he? But no. He didn't turn her way. He didn't blink. He didn't even sigh.

"Should we take notes?" asked Millie, without raising her hand. "Should we write stuff down so we can be sure to do exactly the right the thing for these chicks?" Her heart raced as she waited for Ms. Fritz to say, *Yes, Millie, yes! You're right! This is urgent! Things are getting desperate! Everyone else in here is irresponsible! Please, write things down!*

But instead, Sam said, "Embryos."

"Sorry, Sam?" said Ms. Fritz. "You said something?"

Sam didn't look at Millie. He sat stock-still at his desk, his hands resting in front of him, his notebook and pen buried in his backpack by his feet. But he said *embryos* clear as day. "They're *embryos*, not chicks."

There was a sharp, unfamiliar edge in his voice. Millie didn't understand it. Why was she the bad one, just for wanting a whole bunch of eggs to turn into actual chicks? For caring about all this?

"Ah, indeed," said Ms. Fritz. "Good catch from the son of a science teacher! OK, so we don't get off track, let's all get with our groups and gather around our boxes. That way, when we talk about turning, and about candling, we can actually do something; we can actually practice these things right then and there instead of just talking about them. Yes?"

When Ms. Fritz said yes, with a question mark, everyone knew to say *yes* in response and then walk to the back of the room and check on their boxes. She was that kind of teacher—the kind who didn't have to be mean, because everyone listened to her, everyone nodded and agreed with her, no matter what. That's how Millie *knew* that Ms. Fritz could get everyone to wake up and do a better job if she really wanted to. If she told them to quit horsing around, to take notes, to care. But when Reuben sucker-punched Noah on the way to the back? No reaction. Honestly, it was just chaos in here! And Millie wished again that she'd been put in Mr. Clark's class, where she was sure there was no sucker-punching allowed. Not to mention, no silent treatments. And no Sam.

Instead, here she was, part of the Egg-ceptionals, standing over their box, where six mysterious eggs were at rest, six eggs that had probably been turned all willy-nilly by Nicholas or something.

But, the light was on. Check.

The temperature was exactly 99.5 degrees. Check.

The eggs were nestled safely in their straw bed. Check.

In other words, everything was as it should be.

"Things look . . . OK," said Millie.

Eliza didn't answer. Sam didn't answer, either. Millie wasn't surprised.

"Where's the marker?" said Eliza. "Should I mark the eggs, like Ms. Fritz said? Or do you want to, Sam?" She didn't bother asking Millie, and before anyone could respond, she had the cover off the box and was reaching in to grab the first egg.

"Wait!" Millie's voice sounded like an alarm.

"Seriously?" said Sam and Eliza at the exact same time. Sam had the marker in his hand, but there was a pause then—as big as a breath—when none of them made a move or a sound. Millie could feel other eyes—all the eyes in the room—on them. On her. And then Sam broke the spell, kind of shaking his head, and, for just a moment, she saw something that looked like an ache in his face and down around his shoulders. He looked almost sad instead of mad. Not that it really mattered either way.

"OK, let's go ahead and get 'er done," he said to Eliza, so Eliza picked up the eggs one at a time and handed them to Sam. He slowly—perfectly, even—marked an X on one side of each egg and an O on the other. The symbols really did look like they were exactly opposite each other even though eggs don't technically have sides.

"Good job," said Millie, trying to sound enthusiastic, trying to sound like a team player. But it was too late and she knew it.

So she just whispered "Good job" again, and then, "warmth and light," while Sam and Eliza finished marking the eggs so they could turn them each day—not all Nicholas-ly, but carefully—and *know* that they'd turned them perfectly. Maybe they really would keep those tiny helpless baby chicks alive.

Well, OK, those embryos.

Chapter 20

The walk home from school is longer when you're alone. Millie could've stopped for a candy bar or something, but she didn't want to accidentally run into Sam and have a repeat of what happened in class, so she just headed home.

As she got closer to the top of the hill, she grew more and more worried that Mr. Acosta would appear outside his house, the way he had last time, like a magician—now you see him, now you don't. Or maybe not like a magician; maybe more like a magician's rabbit or the ace of spades or a magic scarf. And the magician was Lolo. Lolo and her light. Mr. Acosta had appeared on a beam of Lolo's light, landing right in front of her like a bird might, landing and humming and swirling and spinning . . . or maybe it had been Millie herself spinning, her ideas and worries and memories and mistakes, spinning like a kaleidoscope—all lit up and dizzying until she believed it, every blinking glimmer of it.

She could not go through it again. She could not see him again and say something dumb and random about bioluminescence that wasn't really dumb and random at all, but he didn't know that. She could not talk to him about Lolo, but she could not *not* talk to him about Lolo, either. Millie worried, and the more she worried, the faster she moved, until she was running, her backpack bouncing off her shoulders and slamming back down against her spine—the big, blue binder inside hitting her hard and flat—like someone was trying to help her clear her throat, like she was choking and needed help to breathe. *Slam, slam, slam,* Millie ran up and past the Acostas', past the magic and the rabbit and the dizzying kaleidoscope of light. She didn't pause to look, not even for a second.

The truth was, she didn't need to. She knew it was on and shining golden from the inside. Like a jellyfish or a glowworm. And she wanted, more than anything, for that to be Lolo, producing and emitting something hopeful and promising, something to believe in. She wanted that more than anything, but it didn't seem to matter anymore. The light seemed to be losing its power.

Millie didn't stop running till she got to her own front door, which she opened and shut in a quick, breathless gasp. It was dark and quiet in the front hall. The only thing turned on inside *this* house was the slow cooker. Millie could smell garlic and ginger over the smell of dogs and breakfast dishes. It smelled good, but everything else was dark and quiet and a little lonely.

She was still panting as she made her way to the kitchen calendar, to see when her mom would get home. Six o'clock.

Six was literally hours from now. Her eyes skipped ahead. Another appointment with Deena the Family Therapist. And then another. And then "Girls with Tad" written across a whole weekend. Millie's life was blocked out in chunks of time spent with people she didn't want to spend time with.

"I'm not going," Millie said to nobody. "I'm not going to Deena's and I'm not going to Dad's. I'm staying here with Mom. And with you guys," she said to the dogs as they pushed through the pet door to say hello. "And with the eggs . . . or chicks. Whatever they'll be by then." The dogs wiggled and panted and jumped on her, as if she'd been gone for a million hours instead of eight. They confirmed that no way, no how, would she be getting on that train and going to Chicago later this month—even if Mom doubled down on the M&Ms.

"Daddy doesn't need me, right, Boo? Right? He's got Silver. You need me, right Leddy? Right, Hazel? Right?"

The dogs shook and wiggled in a way that said, *Yes, yes, you're right. You're right about everything, Millie Donally*, and for that brief blink of a moment, Millie *felt* right. The dogs and the ginger and the garlic and the shimmery gray light pressing up against the kitchen window all felt right—almost magically right. Then the phone rang.

"Hello?" Millie kept rubbing the dogs and they kept wiggling.

"Ah, hello. Is that Ms. Donally?"

"No. Ms. Donally is my mom," said Millie.

"All right, then. May I speak with her, please?" The voice sounded familiar.

"She's not available at the moment," which is secret code for "she's not home," which you're not supposed to say to strangers even though Millie was pretty sure everyone including strangers actually knew that code. Plus, this wasn't a stranger. Was it?

"All right, can you let her know Mr. Rockwell called, from school?"

Oh, Mr. Rockwell! The counselor! Um, why was Mr. Rockwell calling?

"OK," said Millie. She wanted to say *Yes, and . . . ?* as if this were improv, as if it were funny, but she didn't. And she didn't write it down on the message board either. Because deep down, she knew that this had something to do with her, and things that had to do with her were, as a rule, not going too well lately. Plus, Mr. Rockwell, aka Guidance Guy, was not a fave, even on a good day. Like, people dressed up as him for Halloween. As a joke. Millie was pretty sure no good could come of him talking to her mom about anything. So she hung up the phone, went hunting for a snack, and worked to erase the call from her memory.

"Moving on," she said to the dogs as the light from inside the fridge poured out like cream. "That's what I'm supposed to be doing, right? Moving on?" But she shivered a little when she said it, and then double-checked the back door to make sure it wasn't letting the wind in.

Millie watched a show and then did a little homework and was in the kitchen getting more grapes when her mom walked in from work, keys dangling from her mouth, arms full of a purse, a laptop, and two grocery bags.

"OK, Millie," she said, as if they'd been in the middle of a conversation. She dropped the keys from her mouth onto the kitchen counter. "OK," she said again, "let's talk." Lucy walked in behind her, slipped off her backpack, and went running for the bathroom.

There was something about her mom starting like this, so abruptly, instead of saying, "Hey gang? Who's got homework? Who's fed the dog? Who's gonna set the table?" that made Millie nervous and suspicious, and she knew of what: Guidance Guy.

The dogs ran toward Mom, the keeper of kibble, like dinner might actually be *in her pockets*, but Mom ignored them, pushed past them, and came toward Millie. Without so much as a peek in the slow cooker, or at the mail, or anything.

"Sweets, come here. Let's sit down," she said, and she steered Millie toward the couch in the other room. "And where's Tess, do you know?"

"She called to say she was studying with Lila," Millie said, and she felt a little blip of relief that maybe this—whatever *this* was—was about Tess instead of her. Or maybe Mom just wanted to hear about school and lunch and Mr. Brustein's latest joke. Maybe she just wanted to sit and breathe and laugh together. Maybe she wanted to cuddle, to run her long fingers through Millie's hair and along her scalp and spine. That's what Millie wanted, at least, but there was something else in her mom's eyes.

"OK, she's with Lila. Great. Good to know," said Mom. "Now, Millie, here's the deal. I'm realizing I'm in over my head here. I've asked your dad to come out tonight so we can talk, the three of us. I've tried to give you and get you the help and support that you need, but I'm outmatched. This is big, tough stuff, this Lolo stuff, and I'm usually good at big and tough, but . . . honey, you need more than me right now."

She had both of her hands on Millie's knees and she looked steadily into Millie's eyes and she sounded calm, but she looked really, really sad.

"Um, what?" asked Millie. "What are we talking about here?" Even though she was pretty sure she knew.

"You're not doing well, Mills. And I get it. I get it completely. But I don't know how to help you get to the next stage."

Lucy popped out of the bathroom and said, "Wait, what? What is Millie not doing well?" It was almost like she'd been trained by Tess to appear at the most annoying moment possible.

"Lucy," said Mom, "I'm gonna talk to Millie for a few minutes. You do me a favor and throw the ball around the backyard for the dogs. They're feeling antsy." (At which point the dogs went completely ballistic. And some people think that dogs don't speak human? As if.)

Mom stood up then and headed back into the kitchen. Millie lay down on the couch with a sort of dim hope that getting Lucy outside might distract her mom enough that she'd drop this conversation completely.

"But I want to know what she's not doing well at!" Lucy's voice reverberated as the back door shut behind her.

"Millie, I'm getting a glass of water. Can I bring you one?"

"No, thanks," said Millie, hope extinguished. The conversation was clearly not over. "Mom, I don't want to talk and Dad doesn't need to come out here and who told you I wasn't doing OK? I'm doing OK. Doesn't it seem like I'm doing OK?"

"I got a call from school," her mom answered from the sink. "Mr. Rockwell called. It seems as if several teachers are worried about you. Your science teacher, apparently."

Millie wanted to say, "That's not several," but she didn't. What she said was "Well, she should be worrying about the chicks, not about me!"

"Honey, let's not get off-track." Millie's mom slid back into position next to Millie on the couch. She took Millie's head in her lap and looked seriously into her eyes.

Millie looked away—at the wall, the window, the bookshelf—anywhere but at her mom. She felt her face heat up, her neck prickle, her hair itch. "I'm not off-track," she said, and then she swallowed, her throat thick and dry. "I wish he hadn't called," she said, each word taking the most immense amount of energy. "I'm really not . . . off-track." She slipped her feet off the couch then, and tested them before standing. She felt weak and a little dizzy.

"OK, sweetie. It's OK. I hear you. But what about Sam? We haven't seen him around here in forever. And Tessie says that you two are barely speaking and that he's sad and doesn't know what to do."

"Why is everyone talking about me?" Millie's cheeks burned. She wished they all would forget her name and what she did or didn't do. She wished they would stop reminding her of what she didn't need to be reminded of at all.

"Mills . . . ," said Mom, but Millie didn't want to know what she was going to say next. She just moved out of the room and up the stairs on her weak and dizzy feet, feeling almost ghostlike, as if she weren't touching the railing or hitting the steps. As if she were invisible.

If only.

Chapter 21

Mom left Millie alone up there for a long time, which was what Millie thought she wanted, but it was actually kind of hard, just being with herself like that. She listened to music. She opened up her math homework and stared at the equations till her eyes burned and then closed it again. And she lay on her bed and came up with ways to say sorry to Sam—things she knew she should say but that she probably wouldn't, but that made her feel a little better anyway. Because her mom was right; they were barely speaking.

How had everything gone so, so wrong?

When her Mom finally called her down for supper, Tess was home and Lucy had forgotten her need to butt in on Millie's business. All they had to do was sit together and eat. Even the dogs had gone to sleep in a pile. Things were better. Peaceful.

"OK," said Mom, once everyone had a plate, "let's each share something we've done so far this week." She didn't say, *And let's hustle because your dad will be here in half an hour and it'll be awkward if we're still sitting at the dinner table.* Even though it would most definitely be awkward.

"OK, me first!" said Lucy. "I have really good rhyming songs for almost every times table. And I've memorized them. I mean, not the elevens or twelves yet, but the others. Do you want to hear all of them or just most of them?"

"All," said Millie.

"Most," said Mom.

"Some," said Tess.

"OK, most," said Lucy, and she got started with the twos. By the fives, Millie was regretting her vote. Still, it killed time. The piles of lentils shrank, chairs got pushed back a bit, and Millie was surviving this, little by little.

"Let me think," said Tess, when it was her turn. "Oh! I know. We're reading this book called *As I Lay Dying* in English and it's not that it's that long or anything, but what is going on in William Faulkner's head? I don't even know if the book is good! They spend a million years teaching us how to write clear and concise sentences and then they're like, *Here, read William Faulkner.*"

Mom laughed and looked like she was about to answer, when Millie blurted out, "Why does everything always have to be about death? Could they assign a book about superheroes? Or birthday parties? Or something? No. No, they can't. It's like, here, hatch some chicks—unless they die! Here, read a book about . . . I know . . . dying! By the time I'm in high school, it'll be the prom theme, Dying to Dance or something. Can they never, ever give us a break?"

Mom and Tess and Lucy were silent. They stared at Millie. The dogs stared at Millie. The sun stopped setting and stared through the window at Millie.

"Um, the times tables aren't about death," said Lucy.

"I know," said Millie. "OK, I know. And I'm . . . sorry." Everyone was still silent. Millie swallowed, looked at her mom, and said, with a shaky voice, "So maybe I'm not exactly, *exactly* on track. But it's still not Mr. Rockwell's business or Ms. Fritz's or even Sam's. Sometimes a person wants to be left alone a little. And, also, the teachers *should* take a break from death. That part I really do mean." She put down her fork as the sun dipped down beneath the half curtains behind the table. Dinner, she could tell, was basically over.

Mom reached over and squeezed Millie's hand. "Tessie," she said, "will you clear tonight?"

"But I set! I have to set the table *and* clear it?"

Mom's silent stare meant *Yes. Yes, you have to set* and *clear*. So Tess did, while Mom just sat there holding Millie's hand until, after a good long while, the doorbell rang.

"Daddy!" Lucy ran down the hall, ready to sing the times tables all over again.

"One quick hug," Mom called as she followed Lucy toward the door, "and then I want you upstairs getting ready for bed. Your dad and I are going to talk to Millie in the other room."

"But first," said Dad, "ice cream!" And in he came, big and loud and happy, handing each girl a milkshake from Grogan's. He'd even gotten their flavors right. Had they time-traveled? Was this olden dad, before Silver and Chicago and the weird furry rugs? Before Lolo?

Millie's cup was cold and sweaty in her hand, and she thought, What if it was possible? What if I could turn back time and bring Dad home and keep Lolo alive and not ever have to have another sad conversation about any of it? But just as quickly, the cup slipped through her grip and she barely caught the bottom with her other hand. There was no escaping any of this.

Tess went back to the kitchen to do her homework and Lucy sulked her way upstairs, which left Millie to sink into the middle of the couch, her parents standing awkwardly nearby. Mom finally sat down next to her, but Dad kept standing, looking like he didn't know quite what to do with himself.

"Millie," he said, and Mom waved to the spot on Millie's other side, where he finally sat so they were all lined up like they were going to watch a TV show or something.

"Right. So Millie," said Mom, "we love you. We want to help you. We know you're really struggling and really grieving. It's not surprising. Not any of it."

"Right," said Dad. "Exactly." All three dogs pushed up against him, saying, with their noses and their tails, *We remember you!*

"And we thought . . ." Mom trailed off. Mom only trailed off. Millie looked at her perched on the edge of the couch, still in her scrubs, hair pulled back, eyes tired. She could feel Dad looking, too—Dad, who lived in the city with his fancy furniture; Dad, who had to ring the doorbell when he came to visit his own daughters at his old house. Both he and Millie looked at Mom then, waiting, hopefully, for her to say more, because she was the one who always could and did.

Finally, Millie put her milkshake on the coffee table, snuggled in close to her, and said, "You didn't need to come, Dad. I'm OK."

"Look, Millie," he said, not getting the hint, "we're worried about you. You are so sad and we understand that—the circumstances are very, very sad—but things seem to be getting worse and your schoolwork is suffering and your friendships are suffering. We want to help you get through it." He stopped to cough and Millie hoped that was it—that both of her parents were going to offer these generalized sympathies and then let her go to bed. But no. He had more to say.

"So, let's see," he said. "Some ideas. Let's keep trying the therapist. We can commit to that. Has she suggested journaling, Mills? Oh, and I was thinking about the Acostas. What about going over there to talk to them, to break the ice a little? I think we need some ice broken. We could . . . your mom could go with you. Those are some good ideas, right?"

"My schoolwork is not suffering." Millie's head was hot and prickly again. "And I already saw Mr. Acosta, just the other day, and no, those are *not* good ideas." Journaling? That was probably

Silver's idea. Millie made a little clucking noise to call the dogs away from Dad and back over next to her.

"OK, wait. Let's back up a little," said Mom. "Can we back up?"

"OK," said Millie.

"OK," said Dad.

Mom was in charge again, which was a relief to everyone.

"Does school feel hard right now, sweets?" Mom looked right at Millie—not at Dad, not at the dogs.

Millie did not look back. Her heart felt tight. She was suddenly afraid of crying. Instead, she reached for her shake, took a long suck, and said, "Yes."

"Does it feel hard because of things being kind of . . . off with Sam? Or because of the egg-hatching project? Or because of other teachers or classes or friends or . . . ?"

"Yes," said Millie.

"Oh, I remember the hatching project!" said Dad, like he was back in the game, like this was fun.

"It's horrible," said Millie, pushing up out of the cushions and turning toward him. "It's the actual worst! There are all these fragile eggs and homemade incubators and thermistors and . . . like, we're supposed to be in charge? We're supposed to keep a bunch of chickens alive? We're just kids! Did anyone consider that? That we are kids?"

"Um, OK," said Dad.

"Oh, Millie," said Mom.

And they kind of gave up after that. There were a few quiet hugs but no more good ideas, which was another relief. Millie started back upstairs, but she could hear their low voices behind her—*her* parents in *her* house, talking—and she let herself feel that little flicker, that little beat of hope that he'd stay. That he'd stay and help. That he'd be able to fix things. But she shook it off and kept walking toward her room. Because Millie knew better. Millie was smarter than that.

Chapter 22

Millie walked into school carefully, newly aware of just how many people were keeping an eye on her. Her goal for the day was to go nowhere near anyone, which is hard when the whole point of school is to pack twenty-five kids into every little fluorescently lit space available. By the time the bell rang for science, she felt like she'd been holding her breath for hours. And it didn't help that there was a whole cluster of people around Mrs. Fritz's door, making it so Millie could barely get through.

"What is . . . up?" she said to nobody in particular.

"The sky," said Nicholas.

"Our grades," said Sam, which meant they were on speaking terms again, maybe. Only before Millie could think of something to say in return, he was gone, making her wonder if she'd imagined it in the first place.

"OK, everyone, come in. Settle," said Ms. Fritz. "No need to get all flustered—everyone's doing well so far."

"Are we, though?" said Eliza, apparently starting the day kind of pre-mad. "Are we being graded on teamwork?"

Millie wondered that, too. She felt a little panicky as she craned to see her student ID on the posted list.

"Liza. Not cool," Sam said. "Ms. Fritz says we're good."

"Yes, teamwork counts," said Ms. Fritz, "and yes, you're all doing fine. Nothing to worry about. We can get seated now, yes?"

"Yes," said everyone as they shuffled to their spots around the room.

"OK," Millie said. "OK." And it was. She had a 100 so far. She hoped that meant their eggs were all healthy but she feared it just meant Ms. Fritz was an easy grader. There were a lot of 100s.

"Now, back to our regularly scheduled program," said Ms. Fritz. "Today, we are going to take the important step of candling for the first time." Which made Millie panic all over again. Because of the many things she definitely did not want to do today or ever, candling was number one.

"Who can remind everyone what candling is?" said Ms. Fritz. "Who remembers candling from my intro session?"

Millie remembered.

Ms. Fritz pointed to someone behind Millie. "It's when you check to see if the eggs are good or bad," said Reuben.

"OK, good," said Ms. Fritz. "And how do we do that?" She held up a lamp—an ordinary desk lamp—and a cardboard box—as hints.

"By shining a light on them," said Millie.

"Sorry, Millie, what's that?"

Millie must have spoken aloud. Sort of. Like, her mouth had moved, even if her body was suddenly solid ice.

"By looking through the shells to see if the embryo is viable."

Millie doesn't even turn around to see who'd spoken up in her place.

"That's right. We've got, we hope, a good number of fertile eggs, developing normally. But there will be some that are just infertile—believe it or not, those are called yolkers—and then others we'll call bad eggs or dead germs, sometimes referred to as quitters, where an embryo started developing and then . . ."

"Quit!" said someone.

"Died," said someone elsewhere. Someone named Sam.

"Yes, Sam. That's right. And we need to know that because . . ."

"Because they can explode!" Which was, of course, Nicholas, who followed up his comments with explosive sound effects and laughter.

People really have different ideas of the things they find funny.

"OK, OK," said Ms. Fritz. "Yes. They can begin to decompose and eventually explode. Candling—I like to do it twice during the twenty-one-day incubation period—helps us protect our brooding boxes and our good eggs from all that. Plus, you do not want to experience the smell, I assure you."

Cue the fart jokes.

Millie shut her eyes. Yolkers and quitters? Who came up with this stuff?

"OK, friends!" Ms. Fritz shut things down again. "I think maybe we're needing more action and less talk. Let's move on to the actual candling." At which point there were endless minutes of rearranging and logistics—cardboard boxes being traded across groups, overhead lights being turned off, window shades being lowered. And the whole time, in the growing dark, Millie sat there. Frozen and still in her seat.

Finally, as everyone else gathered in the back of the room, Ms. Fritz appeared next to her desk. "Millie?" she said.

"I don't want to know," Millie said.

"You don't want to know...?"

"I don't want to find out whether some of our eggs are dead."

"Ahhh," said Ms. Fritz. "I see. I get that. It's hard. But the thing is, this is one way we can take care of the eggs that are developing. This is part of being good stewards of the process."

She means being good babysitters, Millie thought.

And right then, someone dropped a light bulb and it smashed into a gazillion tiny pieces that sounded like dried rice flying across the hard linoleum floor. Millie jumped. So did Ms. Fritz. Somebody flicked the overhead lights back on and the spontaneous counseling session between Ms. Fritz and Millie was over. Thank goodness.

"OK, folks, that's the end of the fun and games." Ms. Fritz sounded like she meant it.

Finally, thought Millie.

"For the rest of the period, I expect all business." Nobody answered, but someone grabbed a broom.

That could've been an egg that smashed, thought Millie. She shook her head and made her way to the back of the room, to the incubators, to make sure none had.

"Now, let's refocus our efforts," said Ms. Fritz, as the dustpan of glass was emptied into the trash. "I want you to articulate your plan as a team, to each other, before you do a single thing. Communication is key."

Eliza spoke up right away. She was the communication queen. "So, Sam. What do you say you hand me the eggs, I'll do the candling, and Millie will write down the results?" She was looking at Sam and didn't acknowledge Millie at all, not even with a glance.

This is what had become of the Egg-ceptionals, no matter what the grade sheet said. Millie knew, without anyone pointing it out, that it was all because of her, this cold awkwardness. Eliza may be kind of bossy, but they'd gotten along without so much as a bump since she'd moved here in the third grade, and that included more than one sleepover, a few field trips, and a birthday party at Great America when Eliza assigned everyone a partner, as if they couldn't ride a roller coaster with whoever stood next to them in line. Even then, no problem. Until now.

Millie wanted to try to fix things—she really did. So she took a deep breath and got ready to say, "Sure, I can do that. I can write things down," but Sam answered before she had a chance.

"Yep, sounds like a plan," he said. And that was that.

Millie looked at him from underneath her bangs. She looked very carefully. Looking for that flicker again, that nod. Looking to see if there was anything on his face that said that he missed her. That said he knew she was sorry and she missed him, too.

She wondered, if she held a bright bulb up to his face, if she could see through his shell, what would be there, inside? And to her surprise, he looked back and said, very quietly, "Ready, Mills?"

Millie nodded, and without missing a beat, Sam handed Eliza the first egg. Eliza set it carefully in the hole they'd cut into the top of the box. It was almost like the little stands you could dry Easter eggs on, only this egg wasn't hard-boiled. It balanced there, fragile but solid. Perfectly. Eliza bent down low and close. Millie picked up her pencil. Sam sucked in his breath and held it.

"It's alive!" said Eliza, and sure enough, you could see spidery veins covering the inside surface of the first egg. It was fertile. It was alive.

"Wow," said Millie and Sam at the exact same time, which felt old and familiar and almost impossibly good. Another flicker. Another nod.

"Well, all right," said Sam. "Batting a thousand. The Egg-ceptionals for the win!" He handed Eliza the next egg. And the next one after that. The first three were all fertile. Millie found her breath. Inhale, then exhale. She thawed out. She wiggled her fingers and toes. She marked down all the data in their com-position notebook, and as she did, she felt herself beginning to smile.

Occasionally, kids in other groups said things like "Bummer" and "Oh, no," but Millie didn't let herself look to see who they were or what had happened. The Egg-ceptionals had three alive and fertile eggs—embryos! That's what mattered.

Sam was right. They were batting a thousand. He handed Eliza the next egg.

"Hmm," she said. "So, you guys, this one looks different. Right? Don't you think?" The fourth egg sat poised on the top of the box, and it was a statue egg, dark and heavy—absent of spidery veins.

"What's that?" said Sam, pointing at something in the near-center of the egg, sounding hopeful.

"Remember what your options are," said Ms. Fritz, standing behind them at the bench. "Look at the card in front of you to remember the various options for what you might be seeing."

"Easier said than done since we're not nocturnal!" said Sam. But he held up the laminated card in the dim light being thrown by all the candling boxes and tried to make out the descriptions Ms. Fritz was referring to. He shook his head and pointed at a picture on the card. Eliza and Millie leaned in.

"OK, yeah. It's the shadow of the yolk," said Eliza. "This egg isn't fertile. Right, Ms. Fritz?" She turned the statue egg slowly on its pedestal, just to be sure.

"Right," said Ms. Fritz. "That's right. A yolker. It's OK. To be expected, even. Set that one aside." Just like that. As if it were nothing.

It's not nothing, thought Millie. It's an infertile egg. She watched as Eliza lifted the egg from the stand and set it carefully on the counter, making sure it didn't roll. Even though it wasn't alive. Millie nodded.

"Egg number five, please," Eliza said to Sam, and Sam handed it over. Really gently, Millie had to admit. Both Sam and Eliza were being so very gentle. Why had she been so weird and mad this whole time, when they'd actually been doing their best all the way along? She could see that now.

But when Eliza stood this one up in its little stand, it glowed like a planet in the sky—like Saturn, with a red ring around it.

Eliza held up the card.

"A blood ring," said Sam and Millie at the same time, without even looking at the card. This didn't feel nearly as good as when they'd said wow together, just a few minutes earlier.

"Yes," said Ms. Fritz, suddenly behind them again. "Classic blood ring. Sorry, gang."

The Egg-ceptionals stared at the egg, at the murky shadow of the dead embryo—the one that had started to grow but hadn't survived—and at the dark line of decomposing blood vessels that wrapped around the inside of the egg like a rubber band.

"Darn," said Sam. And he sounded truly sorry.

"Yeah, shoot," said Eliza.

They both turned to look straight at Millie for the first time all day, to see what she was going to do or say.

But Millie just stepped away. She stepped away from the deep red planet of an egg—one step, two steps away from her friends, three steps—away from the days and days and days of

darkness. Ms. Fritz had warned them. She'd said this would happen. But still. Millie found her way back to her desk in the center of the room and she lost herself in her backpack, shuffling
her notebooks and her pencil pouch, pulling her jacket out and
heading for the door, so she didn't have to see what happened
next. So she didn't have to watch as the bad egg was set aside or
the next egg—the final egg—was candled.

If she had, she would have seen another happy web of blood
vessels. She would've seen Sam and Eliza high-five. She would've
felt a little better.

But she was gone.

Chapter 23

Millie could see Ms. Fritz grading papers at her desk after school, but she paused before going in. She didn't really want to hang out in the science room anymore, what with the horrors of egg-turning and candling and everything, but she'd been summoned. Probably because you weren't supposed to just walk out of class before the bell rang. At least that's what she figured she was here for.

"Millie, hi. Thanks for coming by." Ms. Fritz looked across the room without putting her pen down. "I've got good news."

Millie doubted that.

"The egg you missed? The final one? Another fertile egg for the Egg-ceptionals!"

"Oh. That's good," said Millie. "Thanks."

Ms. Fritz smiled, a really big, genuine smile. She put her pen down. "I want you to know, Millie, that from my vantage point things are going really well. This is just what we'd hope for out of a hatching project and, honestly, it's smooth sailing from here on out."

Ms. Fritz was gonna jinx the whole thing, talking like that.

"OK," said Millie. "And what should we do to make absolute sure?" She knew she sounded desperate, but she couldn't help herself. Those eggs were not going to hatch themselves. Or, well, they kind of were, but that wasn't exactly reassuring.

"Oh, Millie," said Ms. Fritz. Millie couldn't help noticing that's pretty much all anyone said to her lately.

Before she could say more, Millie raced ahead. "I mean, what happens to the eggs on the weekends, for example? Do you come every day? Or at least once? And has anything ever gone wrong on the weekends, like not just for *our* eggs, but, like, in the history of your hatching projects? When they've been left alone for too long? It seems like there should be a real plan, right? I guess what I'm saying is, I could be part of that plan. Could I be part of that plan?"

"OK...," Ms. Fritz said, drawing it out long and slow. And then quickly, before Millie could interrupt, she said, "Sure, yes. Why don't you meet me here on Saturday? Great idea. I *do* come at least once a weekend—that's the plan you're referring to—but it would be great to have some company. Thank you."

Millie was relieved, both that there had been an actual plan in place and that she was now invited. Never mind that she'd had to do the inviting herself.

"I'm warning you—I tend to bring donuts! And there will be no candling, I promise." Ms. Fritz laughed a little then, like they were in on some secret chicken joke that was definitely not funny.

But it didn't matter. Millie wasn't looking for funny. She knew that extra egg-turning meant extra time and extra responsibility. She knew it meant no trip to Chicago to see Dad and Silver. She knew it meant she'd gone completely and totally egg-crazy, and she didn't care. It felt right. Plus, she really liked donuts. She nodded. "Yeah. OK. Sounds good," she said.

"How about nine thirty, then?" asked Ms. Fritz. "Does nine thirty work?"

"Yes, OK," answered Millie, suddenly feeling shy, like it was Ms. Fritz's idea instead of her own. Still, it was a good one, a good one she wanted to tell Sam about. But by the time she pushed through the front doors to head home, he was nearly a full block ahead of her and walking fast. His shoulders looked stiff and hunched and he wasn't tossing anything—not a can, not a stone, not a hacky sack. Millie could feel his name in her throat.

But she just swallowed it and walked home alone.

"So, I kind of got myself a job," said Millie at dinner. "I mean, I guess it's a volunteer job, really, but it's helping Ms. Fritz with the eggs on Saturday."

"So, in other words, child labor," said Tess. "Over the weekend. What a great deal!" She nearly spit out her sweet potatoes.

"Tess! Enough, honey," Mom said.

"Wait, what's going on?" said Lucy. "I don't get what you're talking about. I hate it when you guys do this. I hate being left out!"

"You could probably get a job like Millie's, Luce. They're kind of easy to come by!" Tess was still laughing and spitting a little.

Millie barely even flinched. She was going to help with those eggs no matter what Tess thought, no matter how right Tess was.

"Mills, the only thing is, this weekend is supposed to be a Chicago weekend," Mom said.

"Oh! Oh, well, no biggie," said Tess. "We can push that off a few weeks, till the chicks hatch." And just like that, Millie's dumb idea became a good one, even to Tess. How convenient.

"We can?" asked Lucy. "Is that OK? Will Daddy think that's OK?" Lucy actually liked the Chicago weekends, or at least she liked them more than Tess and Millie did. Because, pizza. But Millie decided that wasn't her problem. Lucy would survive, and her mom and dad were the grown-ups. Let them sort it out. She got up and cleared her place and went straight upstairs to sleep without reading even a chapter.

On Saturday morning, as Millie was getting ready to go meet Ms. Fritz, Tess came flying down the stairs, knocking into her and kicking her shoes out of her hands. It had been decided that all three girls could stay home for the weekend. Chicago could wait. But Tess didn't appear to be waiting for anything.

"What the . . . ?" Millie said, regaining her balance.

"I'm late," said Tess. "Sorry Mills, but I'm super late, I lost track of time and I gotta go!" She didn't offer Millie a hand—she just grabbed her bike key off the hook and kept running.

"Late for what?" Millie yelled after her.

"Babysitting," said Tess, and the door slammed.

Millie did not say, *Babysitting? For whom?* She did not say, *No, no, not babysitting, please no!* She did not scream or faint or see stars. She just gathered up her own things, walked to the front door, and stepped into the yellowing autumn.

"Warmth and light," she whispered. "Warmth and light." She kept her head down as she passed the Acostas' and didn't look up till she arrived at school.

"Millie," said Ms. Fritz, as she unlocked the side door of school that went almost straight into her classroom, "I'm so glad you could come. You were right. This ends up being quite a big job for me and it's nice to have help."

"No problem," said Millie. Her voice sounded especially loud in the long, dim, empty hallway.

"So . . ." Ms. Fritz ticked through her keys to find the right one for her classroom while Millie waited quietly. "I know this hasn't felt like the easiest or most fun project for you. . . ."

Millie didn't know if that was a question or not, so she just sort of mumbled, "Yeah. I mean, no."

"So . . ." Ms. Fritz pushed the door open, flicked on the overhead lights, and set her keys, coffee cup, and yes, box of donuts on the table just inside.

"So . . ." said Millie.

"You know, Millie, I don't want to sound cold at all, but these eggs"—Ms. Fritz swept her arm toward all the glowing, humming brooding boxes lined up on the counter at the back of the lab—"these eggs are a science experiment. Several science experiments, actually, in cells and reproduction, and matter and elements. In energy. I mean, you know all this already, right? From our syllabus and discussions?"

Millie nodded, so Ms. Fritz kept going. "And we learn something from every bit of it. Every stage. We learn from the teamwork, and the temperature-taking, and even from the blood rings. All of it is part of this experience."

"Yeah, but I mean, that's not the goal, though, right? Chicks are the goal! Live chicks!" Millie felt like Ms. Fritz was giving up.

"Oh, honey," Ms. Fritz said, and she reached over and gave Millie's hands—both hands—a firm squeeze. It was as if she were a little bit more like Millie's mother than her teacher for a second. "You're right. When a few—or sometimes more than a few—actual chicks hatch, it is great and happy news. It's actually pretty cute news, too!"

Millie smiled, imagining that cuteness.

"But listen. I know . . . I really do understand that you've been through something . . . something really traumatic."

Millie stopped smiling. Ms. Fritz knew. She knew about Lolo.

"And I am so sorry, Millie. I really am. You are still so young, but you are trying to make sense of something very big and ancient and scary. You're trying to process how unbelievably fragile life can be. You are grieving. But I promise you that these"—and she and Millie turned to look at the brooding boxes again—"are just eggs. They are just ordinary eggs in a seventh-grade science classroom. You can give yourself a break. You've got to give yourself a break. You're going above and beyond the call of duty just by being here, but whatever's going to happen will happen in the end."

Millie didn't want that to be true. She started to say so, but her eyes felt full and she did not want to cry in front of her teacher, so she just stood there, nodding, as if she understood or agreed.

"The thing is, Millie, we do our best, but we aren't gods or magicians. We're humans." Ms. Fritz wasn't looking at the eggs anymore; she was looking straight at Millie, straight into her nearly overflowing eyes.

Millie wanted to look away. Everything was too practical and sad. What did Ms. Fritz even mean by "just eggs"? What are "just eggs"? Was a tiny little infant "just a baby"? Millie's eyes wheeled around the room, but she couldn't find anything safe to land on. The warming lights? The towering stack of composition notebooks where each group had carefully recorded all their temperature counts and humidity levels? The eggs themselves? Honestly, every single thing in here may as well have a big yellow CAUTION sign slapped on it saying "Don't get too attached. There is nothing—absolutely nothing—you can really do. Whatever's going to happen will happen." One tear spilled out onto Millie's cheek. She didn't wipe it away.

"Do you get all that, Millie? Do you get that even when you do your very best, you're not in control of what happens in the end?" Ms. Fritz sounded soft, almost tender, when she asked that, as if Millie herself was an egg to be kept safe and warm.

"Yeah. I guess so," said Millie, because what else *could* she say. "I get it," she said, "but I don't like it."

"Oh, honey. I know," said Ms. Fritz.

But did she? Did she really know how Millie felt about candling and blood rings and the other kids treating it all like a joke? No matter how soft her teacher's voice or how yummy her donuts, Millie was pretty sure she didn't. The truth is, *nobody* seemed to know. Millie was alone.

But she said "Yeah" again, for good measure, and then headed to the back of the room, where she set to work turning all the eggs, box by box, from one end of the bench, while Ms. Fritz worked toward her from the other end. Millie did it carefully and well each time. She would show Ms. Fritz that it *did* matter. All of it. How much you cared and how closely you paid attention and how hard you tried.

"So here's something funny, Millie," said Ms. Fritz after a bit. "My daughter is telling me this morning that she wants to be a bug for Halloween, like maybe a ladybug. Which is a sweet idea, right?"

Millie nodded and tried to imagine her teacher with kids, the ones in the frame on her desk. She imagined Ms. Fritz saying *Warmth and light* when she tucked them into bed at night, as she hugged them, or squeezed their hands tightly just the way she'd squeezed Millie's. She imagined her own mom saying it, her own mom, who was pregnant for more than eight hundred days. She imagined Mrs. Acosta rocking Lauren Maria Teresa Acosta and whispering *Warmth and light, warmth and light, warmth and light.*

Did it matter? Was it ever enough?

"But the funny part is . . ." Ms. Fritz went on and on, about how, as a science teacher, she was going to need to micromanage that Halloween costume and make sure it was scientifically accurate. Millie held an egg in her hands and closed her eyes and listened to Ms. Fritz laugh, and, for just a moment, she felt the warmth and light of the room and Ms. Fritz's motherly voice and the image of a little girl in a precisely accurate ladybug costume. She was still worried, yes. But she also felt OK, just for a moment.

If only there could be other moments like this one. If only she could start, little by little, stringing them together.

"Lolo," Millie said, so quietly that Ms. Fritz just kept talking and laughing, and Millie didn't mind. She just took a breath and turned the egg in her hands ever so carefully before setting it back in its warm, bright box.

Let this work, Millie wished to herself. Let this keep on working.

Chapter 24

Each day was a hundred days long in the waiting and the hoping. Each night Millie flicked on her night-light, looked out the window at the glow in the street that she was sure belonged to Lolo, and then got ready for bed with a tiredness too heavy for a twelve-year-old.

Tonight was no different, except for the thunder. That surprised Millie. The sky had been gray and quiet and dry since the weekend, but that was thunder now, for sure—big, booming, serious thunder. She put down her toothbrush to listen.

Yep. There. And there again, each time a little louder and a little closer until finally Millie heard the crackle of lightning, too, and then big fat drops slapping against the windowpanes.

She slipped into bed, flicked on her bedside light, and picked up her book. It was a library book, one she'd checked out when she'd gone back to return the one on bioluminescence, after she'd copied nearly all the important, Lolo-ish stuff into a notebook so she'd remember it forever. When she'd taken it up to the desk to scan it back in, Ms. Marion asked if she'd learned a lot and Millie'd said, "Oh, yes. Like, basically, light is kind of life." Even as she said it, Millie didn't exactly know what she meant, but she knew it made her feel better. Good, even.

"Oh, I like that," said Ms. Marion, and then she moved aside to let Millie check out her new book.

This one was fantasy, with no bioluminescence and also no babysitters. Thank dog. She moved through three chapters fast, almost without realizing she was turning pages, as the backdrop of thunder grew louder and louder until it was kind of part of the story, the hero moving through a portal, her hair (or was it leaves from a weeping willow? was it seaweed?) wet from some storm, and the horse—where had he come from?—whinnying, wet and anxious next to her! *Boom!*

And that's when Millie's light went out. Actually, all the lights in the house went out. Not blinked or skipped or hesitated, but went dark completely. Millie sat there in her pitch-black room. "OK," she said to nobody. She put her book down, swung her knees over the side of her bed, and stood up. She thought she should go find her mom, she thought they should all meet together in the kitchen and get flashlights and candles and stuff, but first she walked to her window and looked out toward the Acostas'. She craned her neck and looked for light, through the rain and the dark night and the trees. She couldn't see Lolo's bedroom from her bedroom, of course, but there should be a glow in the air, right? There was usually a glow in the air—not the sudden, crackly, lightning-strike kind of glow, but the Lolo kind—soft and warm. Right? Millie suddenly couldn't remember what Lolo's light looked like, and she started to panic.

Boom! The thunder just kept coming and the fat drops and the dark—it all just kept coming and coming, punctuated only by the occasional fierce crack of lightning. It grew so, so dark, inside and out, that Millie could hardly see her own hand, pressed against the window, where she stood looking for a bioluminescence that was just plain not there.

And then a cry, winding through the storm—higher-pitched and airy, but almost as strong as the weather. It could have been Lolo crying. It could have been Mr. Acosta, or Mrs. Acosta. But it wasn't. It was Millie crying. Wailing, even. Wailing as her mom held her, wrapped her up tight and said, "It's OK, Millie, it's just a storm. The electricity's out. Everything is OK, I promise."

But it wasn't. As Millie heard herself howl like a creature caught in a trap, she knew the truth. She felt it like lightning in her bones.

"It's not OK!" Her voice was ragged and hoarse. "Nothing is OK! Lolo's gone, Mom. She's gone. Even her leftover light is gone."

She felt her own mom crying with her then. It was as if the whole world was crying because Lolo was really, truly gone. She'd slipped away that night in August, the night Millie babysat for the very first time, and she'd been gone ever since.

"Why? Why," cried Millie. "Why?" The word spilled from Millie like a song, a song in another language, like the hymns sung in St. John's the day of Lolo's funeral. Millie sang and cried and reached one more time toward the window, her eyes straining for anything, some tiny glint of light to tell her she was wrong—that there was hope, that there was something still to hang on to—but there was nothing. It was deep, deep dark. After a few more minutes, even the rain stopped. The storm, as quickly as it had arrived, was over.

When Millie woke in the morning, she was curled up in her mom's bed under the big king-size comforter, just like when she was little and had gotten sick or had bad dreams. Her mom was next to her and Millie could tell she was still asleep by the low whistle she made when she breathed. A little bit of sunshine pushed through the curtains and the dogs nudged their noses up under the covers to make sure Millie knew they were there.

"Yep," Millie said to the noses. "I see you. I see you. . . ." But then she just lay there, remembering last night and the millions of hours leading up to last night. She remembered falling asleep at the creek, and making Deena a clay chicken, and candling their eggs. Remembered her dad coming over with his ice-cream shakes and bad ideas. Remembered the storm and the rain and the lights going out.

Remembered Lolo's light going out.

And it wasn't until then—right then—that she realized that the lights keeping their eggs warm had probably gone out, too.

Millie flew out of bed and kicked past the dogs. In her room, she found yesterday's jeans and a shirt on the floor, she grabbed a hair band from her desk, and she was downstairs and out the door in five minutes. She wasn't worried about breakfast or her backpack or even her mom. She was just worried about those eggs. Those eggs without their incubator lights.

She ran past all the still-dark houses in the neighborhood, including the Acostas'—the darkest, emptiest, stillest house of all. She looked right at it—right into the dark—but she didn't stop. She kept running, and didn't even notice as the sun crept up.

By the time she got to school, she was panting hard and her hair had come undone. The front doors were locked, so she ran around the side to the science wing and just started pounding like her life depended on it. She panted and pounded until from somewhere deep inside, the custodian appeared.

"Whoa, whoa. What's the deal here, champ?" he said. "You gotta chill out. You're gonna break the door down."

Millie looked at the long fluorescent lights lighting up the hallway behind him. "The, um, the electricity . . ."

"Yeah?"

"It's on?"

"Rocket scientist," said the custodian, leaning on the door-frame like he didn't have a care in the world. He was smiling at her.

"Is Ms. Fritz here?" Millie asked, her breath slowing and her voice nearly back to normal. Still, she knew that just because the lights were on now didn't mean that they'd been on all night and didn't mean that the boxes were warm or the eggs were safe. "Y'know, the science teacher?" she said.

"Yep, I know Ms. Fritz. She'll be here soon, I bet. She's one of our early birds. Not quite as early as you, though, huh?"

"I guess not. OK. OK." And she backed away from the door. All the hurry and rattle ran out of her then, through her fingers and toes, until she felt like she could barely stand upright. She circled around toward the front of the school, so slowly, not knowing what to do with herself. "OK," she said again, to herself this time. She figured she'd just sit on the front steps, maybe, until everyone else arrived and she could go in and check for herself, but that's when her mom came peeling into the semicircle driveway like a race-car driver. She threw the brakes on and jumped out, leaving her door open.

"Millie! You terrified me! What is going on?"

Lucy sat wide-eyed in the back seat. Millie had apparently terrified her, too.

"I . . . the eggs. I was worried about our eggs because of the power going out, like were they sitting in the cold and dark all night? But now Ms. Fritz isn't even here, and the power's back on, and . . ." It all seemed dumb and pointless. If something bad was going to happen, it had already happened—last night, during the storm. Millie shrugged.

"Oh, wow. I just don't even . . ." Millie's mom trailed off. She pulled Millie into her and squeezed her tight, as if they hadn't seen each other in years. Then she opened the door to the passenger seat of the car, Millie slipped in, and they headed home to start the day all over again.

As they drove past the Acostas', Millie turned to see what she knew she'd see: every pane of glass still dark, every beam of light snuffed out.

Chapter 25

Even though Millie stopped by the science room three times, she didn't see Ms. Fritz or the eggs until after lunch. Ms. Fritz's door was locked and there was a sign on it that said MORNING IN-SERVICE MEETING—BACK THIS AFTERNOON, which Millie suspected was code for TORTURING MILLIE JUST A LITTLE BIT LONGER.

But then there she was, Ms. Fritz, standing up in front of class, just like always, as if nothing was wrong at all.

"OK, everyone. Listen up . . . ," she said as they filed in after lunch. "Listen up, we've got to get going right away today."

That's when she noticed Millie already had her hand up. "Yep? Millie?"

"Did the power at school go out last night in the storm? Because the power went out at our house and if it went out here, too, and all the lights and heaters and thermistors and everything went out, then does it mean the eggs are all ruined and the chicks are all dead and this whole thing was . . ."

Someone whistled.

Someone else laughed.

Someone, please don't let it be Sam, said, "Dude," in a super-irritated way.

"Millie, Millie." Ms. Fritz held up her hand like a stop sign. Millie stopped.

"Do you know what a generator is, gang?" asked Ms. Fritz.

"Like, a motor?" someone said.

"That generates electricity?" asked someone else.

Millie was glad her classmates were chiming in because she felt like she'd just run all the way to school again. Her heart raced so loudly she could barely hear what they were saying.

"Yep, exactly. And guess what we have here at school? Generators! So, never fear. Your eggs were not without power last night, even if you all were. OK?"

She looked directly at Millie then. Millie nodded. OK. She slowed down from tip to toe. She was relieved. The generators had done nothing to change the utter darkness that had enveloped her neighborhood last night, the dark waves of nothingness that had stretched from the Acostas' house to her house and back again, but at least she felt better about the eggs.

Millie looked over at Sam and caught his eye. He didn't smile, not exactly, but there was a flicker of comfort in his look, a nod that said, *Yep, all's well.* So Millie pretended it was. She floated just a little bit outside her body and watched herself turn eggs and take notes and even try to talk to Sam and Eliza. She watched herself walk up the hill after school and look through the unlit windows at the Acostas'. She watched herself take the dogs around the block and do her math homework and eat spaghetti for dinner.

"How was school, loveys?" Mom passed the salad to Millie.

"Oh. My. Gosh. Mom." Tess put down her fork and pulled her phone out, which was supposedly not allowed at dinner. "Look at the picture the Wynns sent me from Saturday. Cutest. Baby. Ever."

What? No, thought Millie. Not the cutest baby ever!

"He has these chubby arms and legs that sort of stick out when he walks so it looks like he's wearing a marshmallow costume." Tess got up and kind of stick-walked around the kitchen with her arms and legs out, pretending to be the chubby baby.

"Oh, how sweet and funny," said Mom, eagerly taking the phone from Tess. "That was so nice of them to send you a picture. Are they nice? Did they pay well? And will you pass the salad to Lucy, Mills? Lucy—at least three green leaves, right?"

That was too many questions to be answered all at once, plus Millie wanted to ask her own.

"What about Lolo?" she asked, right as Tess was saying, "Yes! They paid really well. I'm rich!"

"What?" said Mom and Tess and Lucy all at once. Mom put her fork back down.

"What about Lolo? Wasn't she the cutest?" Millie felt her pulse speed up. She felt frantic, like she had to make sure nobody forgot Lolo.

"Um, yes?" said Tess. She looked at their mom for some assistance.

"Oh, Millie. Of course. Tess wasn't saying this baby was any cuter than Lolo. She was just saying . . ."

"She *did* say he was the cutest baby ever," said Lucy, who was digging into her pasta with no sign of stopping for a breath or bite of salad. "I heard her."

Millie caught Lucy's eyes and tried to telegraph a thank-you. Not for taking sides, exactly, but for paying attention.

"OK, but that isn't what Tessie meant. Millie . . ." Mom looked so sad all of a sudden.

Tess jumped in before Mom could finish. "I was just excited about my new job! Is a person allowed to be excited about anything around here? Is that still a thing?" And then she made kind of a growly "Argh," like she couldn't even deal with Millie anymore, but Millie could tell there was a lump in her throat.

"Right," said Mom. "So let's move on. Let's see . . . Oh! The eggs! Millie, I've wondered all day . . . how were the eggs? After the storm and everything?"

"Fine," said Millie quickly. "They're just eggs," she said, and she sounded so casual, so whatever, that for a second she almost believed herself. As if she hadn't left the house under the cover of darkness this morning like some sort of panicky poultry superhero.

"Good. That's so good," said Mom, and she smiled at Millie, obviously willing to forget this morning, too.

Millie smiled back gratefully, and then she said, "I think we should have the Acostas over for dinner. Y'know, sometime." Also casually. As if it were a perfectly normal, everyday idea.

Her mom's mouth fell open. So did Tess's. Millie was a little surprised herself, honestly, but she was also just plain tired. She was tired of moving past the Acostas' house as quickly and invisibly as she could. Tired of wondering about them. Tired of worrying about them. And about Lolo. And about Lolo's light. She was tired of being all wobbly and nervous every day, but as soon as she said the words *we should have the Acostas over*, they made her wobbly and nervous, too. She shoved a bite of food into her mouth to keep from taking them back.

Mom finally broke the silence—everyone else just sat there snarfing spaghetti like it was the last food on Earth. "OK," Mom said. "Well, that's a lovely idea. A brave and lovely idea. I'm not sure . . . I mean, let's think about the timing, right? And make sure . . . that we're . . . ready?"

"Yep," said Millie, her mouth full. She was relieved that her mom said yes, and also relieved that it might not happen right away.

In fact, days went by and nobody mentioned the dinner idea again. But absolutely everyone mentioned the eggs. It was like Millie's obsession had become dangerously contagious. Tess asked almost every afternoon—she said she had a "vested interest" since she'd helped build the brooding box and she felt that they were partly her chicks, too. Millie would give her a few updates and then hold out her hand to stop Tess from asking anything more. "That's it," she'd say. "That's all I know."

Dad asked about the eggs, too, in an email and two texts that Millie didn't answer, and even Deena the Family Therapist suddenly took a great interest. (Millie was not surprised to find herself back at Deena's so soon after the whole storm situation.)

"Now, Millie," said Deena, "your mom tells me you've got kind of a high-pressure science experiment going on at school right now. With eggs?"

Millie knew where Deena was going with this and she hereby regretted inviting Tess to help build the Egg-ceptionals box. She regretted volunteering in Ms. Fritz's room at lunch and on the weekends. She regretted ever mentioning this dumb, hard, scary project to anyone.

"Not really," she said. "I mean, yes, but it's not like it's that big of a deal or anything." Millie wiggled around in her seat, pretending she meant what she said. Pretending she was Ms. Fritz, or Sam, or even Nicholas. All nonchalant. But she was chilly and damp from running into the office through the rain. Just in case it wasn't uncomfortable enough going to therapy when you were dry.

"Oh, well, good. That's good." Deena sounded happy about Millie's lie. She pushed the modeling clay across the table, maybe hoping for another little statue. "So, the embryos are all OK?"

Chicks, Millie thought.

But she said, "No." That was the end of her nonchalance. She could not stand the clay or the worry stones or Deena's weird, serious, uncomfortable skirts and sweaters anymore. She could not stand the questions. And not just Deena's, either. She could not stand all the questions from all the adults who didn't have any good answers themselves.

"No?" said Deena.

"They're not. The chicks are not OK. I'm not OK. School is not OK. Lolo is not OK. Nothing is really OK." She was loud by the end—loud like the storm outside her bedroom window the other night. Loud and dark as the storm.

"Oh, Millie, you sound really upset," said Deena. "You sound . . . mad?"

Millie *was* mad. She was mad from the inside, from her belly, like there was a fire she could not put out. But it was made of more than mad. Millie was mad and scared and tired and lonely and . . . desperate—absolutely desperate—to fast-forward through this. So it could all be over—the appointments with Deena, the stalemate with Sam, the chicken-hatching project, and the constant sorrow and guilt over little Lolo Acosta.

"And when you say Lolo is not OK," said Deena, "you mean . . . ?"

Millie felt something unhinge in her then, the little lock that had been holding her hopes and secrets in place. "I mean that she is really gone," said Millie. "The luminescence was like some sort of . . . I don't know . . . optical illusion or something. Her light has gone off. It was always on before, and now it's off, and there's nothing I can do about it."

"OK," said Deena. "Her light ... I'm trying to catch up here ..."

"It doesn't matter," said Millie. "The point is, it's dark now. I have to focus on other things."

"Other things? Like what?" Deena was rolling a little chunk of the clay between her own fingers now.

"Like the eggs," Millie said, in a high, thin voice that said they were a big deal after all.

It was silent then for a moment. Deena the Family Therapist just sat there, in her maroon suit and lipstick with a glossy lump of clay in her hands. It looked not unlike an egg, actually. Millie wondered if she had stumped her. She kind of liked that maybe she had.

But then Deena said, "Millie, I am so sorry. You are holding a lot. A lot of big, heavy stuff. I'll bet you just wish you could set it all down sometimes."

And Millie thought, Yes, that's kind of it. Deena kind of gets it.

She reached out for a piece of clay then, and pressed her thumb into it, leaving her own personal impression. And she spent the rest of the appointment not talking so much as just feeling understood.

Chapter 26

Mr. Brustein's homeroom felt longer than forty-five minutes. Was it because of the gray flannel sky of morning, or Luisa's endless blather, or Mr. Brustein's bad jokes? It's hard to say. All of those things, probably. But mostly, Millie knew, it was long because of Sam kind of avoiding her still. This was a long and sad and tortuous thing, not having Sam at her side, and it made every moment seem like a mile.

Millie would catch his eye sometimes now. She'd smile. She'd refer to him in a group, like "Oh, Sam is good at that" or "Let Sam decide!" But he never really cracked. Not completely. It was like everything that was familiar about him—his jokes and his energy, his way of being Sam—had been walled off or shut down or locked up tight. It was as if his light had gone out—just like Lolo's—and Millie was responsible for this loss, too.

Today she sat on the other side of the room so it didn't seem so obvious that they weren't themselves, a pair, Sam and Millie. It wasn't easy, but it wasn't really any harder than anything else she had to do to get through a day—tending to the eggs, talking to Deena, walking by the Acostas' house morning and night. Maybe this is what Mr. Acosta meant when he said, "We are moving through our days." Maybe that's exactly what she was doing.

"All right folks, because we have a few minutes before the bell rings," said Mr. Brustein, "did you hear about the new restaurant on the moon?"

He was answered by a giant, class-size groan. They didn't even pretend to be entertained anymore. Poor Mr. Brustein. He tapped his marker on the whiteboard—*tap, tap, tap*—to build suspense. *Tap, tap, tap.*

"OK," said Marcus. "We give up. What's with the new restaurant on the moon, Mr. B?"

Mr. Brustein beamed. Millie thought he might actually walk over and hug Marcus for playing along. But instead he just beamed, stopped tapping, and said, "It's got great food, but there's no atmosphere."

"*Ba-dum-chhh.*" That was Sam. A little tiny flicker of the old Sam, sound effects and all. Millie knew it—his voice in her ears like a secret—but she didn't dare look up or over. She didn't dare laugh. But she did smile a little smile to herself, and it felt good.

"Thank you, thank you. I'll be here all week." More groaning. Mr. Brustein put down the marker and sat on the edge of his desk. "OK, folks, I can share the limelight. Who else wants to go? Millie? Weren't you our comedy camper?" He zoomed in on her like a spotlight, like it actually almost burned her skin, the way he looked at her. Millie, in the limelight, telling jokes aloud?

Now, *that* was laughable. Comedy camp was as long ago as the Big Bang, she thought, and there was not a single chance of this new, non-star-like Millie conjuring up anything that even half-way resembled a joke.

And then the bell rang.

"Darn! Why does time just fly?" said Mr. Brustein to the backs of a whole bunch of relieved and fleeing seventh graders.

But what Millie wondered was, Why *doesn't* time fly? Why can't Monday be Friday? Why can't the eggs hatch and the chicks grow up and start laying eggs of their own? Why can't fall become winter? Why can't Sam be Sam again? Why can't seventh grade become eighth grade, and thirteen become fourteen and then fifteen and then sixteen? Why can't these dark, rainy days of autumn just fly by, quickly, into the ancient past?

She could see—by looking all the way down the hall and out the glass doors at the end—the wind whipping the autumn leaves into little tumbleweed dervishes, as if trying hard to fly by at that very moment, right on cue.

When Millie peeked into the science room over lunch, Ms. Fritz waved but didn't say, *Come in!* Instead, she said, "Y'know, Millie, you don't need to hang out with them today. All is well— and you're pulling double duty already, what with your new weekend shift. You can relax a little, remember? Go be a kid for a bit!"

Ms. Fritz had her shoes off and was eating a sandwich at her desk. And it was an egg salad sandwich, of all things. *Egg* salad! Really, Ms. Fritz?

Millie understood that Ms. Fritz was basically banning her. Kicking her out. She understood that this was the teachers' lunch break, too, and that Ms. Fritz had had Millie on her hands for weeks, whether she'd wanted her or not. But where was Millie supposed to go? Not to the cafeteria, where Sam would be sitting with Eliza and Anna and Dante and Bonnie and whoever'd taken her spot. Not to the bathroom because honestly, how much time can you spend in the bathroom unless you're one of those girls who really likes reapplying mascara? And not home, thanks to the State of Illinois truancy laws, although that's the option Millie preferred by far.

But then she thought of Ms. Marion. Did she have a good excuse to go back to the library? Did she need one? She hadn't finished the novel she'd started the other night, but . . . could she do some research? Or maybe she had a deep and sudden need for hummus and pretzels? Or could she just shrug when Ms. Marion asked what she was looking for and say, "Books"?

Millie pushed into the library. The babysitting display was down, thank dog, replaced by one on asteroids and black holes and poor Pluto, that sorry sometimes-planet. Millie reached for the laminated article at the front of the display and stood there, reading. It was quiet in the library, and only the lights in the back by the circulation desk were on. Nobody interrupted her. Nobody heard her when she said, out loud, "Huh. Maybe black holes are the opposite of luminescence."

By the time Ms. Marion returned, Millie knew that black holes happened when stars died and collapsed in on themselves. She knew they threw up such intense gravitational fields that no light could ever escape them. She knew they could devour the things around them. And Ms. Marion stepped into the middle of all this discovery, flicked on the overhead lights, and said, "Oh! Hello, Millie. I'm so sorry—I had to run to the office and I didn't know anyone was here! Welcome!"

Millie blinked. "Um, thank you?"

"What can I do for you?" Ms. Marion walked right past Millie with a stack of papers and books in her arms, but she turned and looked at her and smiled as she did. It was nice.

"Did you know black holes trap light? That's why they're called black holes." Millie followed Ms. Marion and kept talking. "They are strong forces. They can bend time!" Millie didn't know what she wanted Ms. Marion to say. She didn't know why this mattered. But it did.

Ms. Marion put down her stack of things. She turned her whole body toward Millie and looked her square in the eye. "You," she said, "are very interested in light and dark. Aren't you?"

"Yes," said Millie. "I really am." And she leaned forward, almost as if she might hug Ms. Marion, or collapse in her arms. But instead she just said, "Thank you, Ms. Marion."

Chapter 27

As soon as Millie walked into science class, she understood why Ms. Fritz had kicked her out at lunch—and it wasn't so she could eat her mean-spirited egg sandwich in peace.

On the whiteboard, in block letters, was one word:

CANDLING.

Today was their last chance to check to see if all their eggs were still viable. Day seventeen. After this, the chicks would be too big to even see properly inside the eggs. After this, they'd need to be left alone to finish developing in peace. After this was lockdown—when nobody would be allowed to touch the eggs or even be allowed to open the incubators till the chicks hatched. This was it.

Millie knew that Ms. Fritz hadn't invited her in at lunch because she did not want her freaking out until the last possible minute. It was like when Tess and Millie were little—before Lucy was even born—when their mom would have them nearly inside the pediatrician's office before admitting to them where they were going and why. (Spoiler alert: shots.) The freakouts were just as bad as they would've been, but shorter. Less of a lead-up. That's what Mom said. And Ms. Fritz was obviously just as sneaky.

Millie sucked in all the air she could handle. Candling. Again.

"Ooooh, Millie's favorite," said someone.

"I am going to presume," said Ms. Fritz, ignoring the chatter, "that you already know what to do this time around and that there won't be any more broken bulbs. Am I right?"

"Yep," said everyone except Millie, who was still holding her breath. She looked toward the back of the room, where all the incubators were lined up next to each other, awash in their own warm buzz, and she imagined for a moment that it was bio-luminescence: that the light came from the eggs themselves; that the eggs were producing and emitting light; that the kids on either side of her—Sam and Eliza, Nicholas and Kat and all the others—were not kids, but coral; that the air was water, pulsing with living light. Waves and waves of warmth and light.

"OK, and I'd like someone else in your group to do the actual candling this time," Ms. Fritz added. "You always want to make sure you're rotating responsibilities, so that by the end, you've each learned a little bit about everything and you all have deep ownership in the project at hand."

"I can do it," Millie said, under her breath. She didn't really want more ownership—she felt so much already—but her voice grew in her throat, it reached out, the way it had in Deena the

Family Therapist's office the other day. She heard herself say, "I can do it" again, and she knew it was true—she could, she could do it, even if she didn't want to. Even if she *really* didn't want to.

"Yeah. You can. You totally can," said Sam. The old Sam, the Sam who used to know her and love her, the Sam she'd shouted at and who still, somehow, was standing right next to her with a voice that pulled her, carried her like a boat, across the classroom, toward the eggs, the hum, the light.

And there, Millie did what she needed to do. She did what the Egg-ceptionals needed her to do. Eliza handed an egg to her, and when she shined the light through the shell, it was nearly black—filled up with chicken, much more chicken than the last time they'd done this!

And then another—the same thing. A chick. Alive.

"Like a black hole," she said. "So dark, but so full and dense and powerful."

"Um, yeah." Both Sam and Eliza agreed, even though Millie could tell they had no idea what she was talking about. But it didn't matter. She was doing this. *They* were doing this. They were candling the eggs and it was OK. It was actually kind of cool. They were raising real live chicks.

The third egg was different. Millie could still make out the shiny veins near the bottom, but that just meant this chick was smaller than the others. Still alive, but taking up less room.

"We've got a runt!" said Sam. "I love runts!"

"You are a runt, dude!" called Nicholas, and everyone laughed. Millie handed their runt back to Eliza, who set it gently, gently back into the incubator.

"OK, good," said Millie. And then she smiled an actual, genuine smile at Sam—a smile full of thankfulness, not just for today, for giving her one more, unexpected chance, but for the day she fell asleep by the creek with the dogs, for the times he'd stopped by to check on her even though she wouldn't come to the door, and for everything—everything!—before all that. The pet funerals and grilled cheese sandwiches and April Fools' Day jokes. Things had not been OK for a long time now—not with her, and not with her and Sam. But as she smiled a smile of apology and gratitude at him, she knew it was never too late.

Eliza handed Millie the fourth egg. She liked the weight of it in her hands. It was warm, like the others. She held it up against the light, like the others. But there, like a severe storm on the Weather Channel, was a blood ring.

They had lost another embryo. The Egg-ceptionals were down to three viable eggs—just half the number they'd started with. Three viable eggs and three days left.

Millie didn't say anything. Neither did Eliza. Neither did Sam.

She just set the egg aside and thought of everything she'd messed up lately, everything she'd tried to do right, everything she'd loved as hard as she could but had lost anyway. Millie sighed, but she didn't cry. She wasn't mad and she wasn't surprised. She was just really, really sad. Maybe that's what she'd been this whole time, even when it felt like anger and fear and worry and all that other stuff.

When the last bell rang, she slipped out of school and walked home quickly—past the mini-mart, past the Acostas' house without looking to see if the windows were light or dark. Because bioluminescence, she now knew, was like love or hope. It needed something living and breathing behind it, to make it real. To make it shine. And black holes were like grief. They were like storms that left you powerless. They could swallow light.

Chapter 28

"I wanted to tell you," said Millie, when her mom came in say good night, "I don't really mind Deena the Family Therapist after all." Her voice was strong.

Her mom looked surprised. "OK, honey. Well, that's good. I'm glad."

"Yeah." Millie pulled her covers up all the way to her chin. "She's not as bad as you'd think."

Mom laughed a little, but she didn't say, I didn't think she was bad. Or, I told you so, Millie. Or anything like that. She just said, "I'm really glad," and then she smoothed Millie's hair and kissed the top of her head three times.

Millie did not think Deena was perfect. She wished she were a little bit more like Ms. Marion, with less lipstick and more pretzels, less talk and more books. But everyone helped in their own way. And Millie had both Ms. Marion and Deena the Family Therapist. And Ms. Fritz and Tess and even Sam. Deep down, she knew that.

"I'm really glad, too," she said.

"Sleep tight, my sweets," said Mom, flicking on the night-light for Millie before she shut the door behind her.

And Mom, thought Millie. No matter what, I have my mom. She fell asleep easily, then, as the forever rain tip-tapped up on the roof.

For the next couple of days, it rained in earnest. Millie went back and forth to school in a kind of a watery, rain-coated daze. Each day, Sam would give her the countdown when she arrived in homeroom. "Day nineteen," he'd say, or "Day twenty," and Millie would smile or give him a thumbs-up. It was a weird, quiet, partial truce—it wasn't like they were hanging out again, not really, or that Sam was back to doing spot-on imitations of her dogs and sending flying hacky sacks her way, but he was softening a little bit, maybe partly due to the weather and the waiting.

"Honestly, this fall!" said Mom on Thursday morning. "I've about had it with all the wet, gray days." She poured another cup of coffee and set a few cereal boxes out on the kitchen table. Lucy let the dogs in from the backyard and they shook their matted wet fur, lazily. They had had it, too.

"Girls, I'll drive everyone to school today on my way to work, sound good? Nobody wants to start the school day soaking wet." She brushed some dog fur from her scrubs and shook her head.

"Nobody actually wants to go to school at all," said Millie. Tess fist-bumped her for that, like it was a joke. But Millie wasn't joking. She was nervous. Maybe even more than nervous. She was scared. She knew what day it was today.

"Yeah, yeah. Smart alecks. Come on, if you want a ride, you'll have to hustle." Mom led the way, and within minutes they'd all piled into the car, including Lucy, who normally took the bus down the hill. Mom stopped at each school—elementary for Lucy, then middle for Millie. Tess was about to hop out, too, when Mom said, "No, no, honey—I'll drive you across the parking lot. Door-to-door service!" And away they went.

Millie walked so slowly toward the front of the school that she was all drippy by the time she got inside, never mind her mom's good intentions. Please, Mr. Brustein, no jokes today, she thought. Please, please. She slipped into homeroom and stuck herself wetly to her seat.

And then, there was Sam—not wet at all; he got door-to-door service every day since his dad brought him—and he was not only dry, but smiling. An honest-to-goodness, genuine Sam Clark smile. "Guess what today is?" he said. And then he answered before giving her the chance: "Day twenty-one."

In spite of herself, Millie smiled back. "Day twenty-one," she said.

"This is what we've been waiting for!" he said. "Today . . ." and before he could finish, before Millie could agree with him, before Mr. Brustein could crack even the beginning of yet another joke, Ms. Fritz came busting through the door.

"Mr. Brustein, can I borrow a few of your students? Millie? Sam? Is Eliza in a different homeroom? Can you guys come with me?" Then she turned and ran back out of the room as quickly as she'd come in.

"Dude!" said Sam, reaching out to grab Millie by the hand. "Come on! Seriously! I think we've got action!"

So there was Millie, on her feet, following—no, leading—Sam down the hall. She was pulling him, running—flying—toward the science room! Ms. Fritz and Eliza came running, too, from the other direction, arriving at the same time she and Sam did. And Ms. Fritz? Ms. Fritz was beaming—like she had been on the first day of school. She looked like there was nothing more thrilling in the world than the hatching of a chick.

And, honestly, that's because there kind of isn't.

It is quiet. It is slow. But it is thrilling.

Sam and Eliza and Millie and Ms. Fritz stood over their beautiful handmade brooding box that was, they all knew, an absolutely perfect 99.5 degrees, and together they watched the first of their three eggs go from pip to chick.

"When I arrived this morning, it had already made a good start," said Ms. Fritz, in almost a whisper. "I think your little one had a long night!"

And sure enough, the egg was cracked on one side—not completely open yet; there was a thin, skin-like membrane still between the outside and the inside of the egg, but that membrane was see-through. And through it, they could see movement. Shapes. Feathers.

They could see their chick!

Their hard-working, very-much-alive chick. Pushing. Twisting. Poking. Resting.

And finally, popping a hole all the way through.

That's when it really got wild, because that crazy chicken started using her whole body—her rounded back, her sharp feet—to push the rest of the egg apart. She looked desperate—and who wouldn't be? After all those days wrapped up tight! She kicked and thrashed and, wow, it was a lot.

But then—in an instant—there she was! Her feathers wet. Her skin pink. Her body tired. She was hilarious and sort of creepy-looking and strangely beautiful. She was born!

"Oh my dog!" said Millie, in a voice like a bell. As clear as day. The others laughed and clapped and started cheering.

"Oh my dog, indeed," said Ms. Fritz.

"We did it!" said Millie.

"We did," said Eliza and Sam. And as the gray rain came down outside the windows, the Egg-ceptionals watched their chick stretch and reach and flop and rest after her hard, long journey. And their attention turned to egg number two, where another glorious pipping had already begun.

"Bioluminescence," said Millie, and even though nobody knew what she was talking about, they all nodded. And then, because they already seemed agreeable, she added, "Warmth and light."

And Sam said, "Eggs-actly."

Chapter 29

By the time school let out, there were ten newly hatched chicks, warming and resting in brooding boxes all across the back of the science room, plus more on the way, and a whole lot of happy seventh graders. The rain had stopped. And Sam walked out with Millie like the old days, like normal, as if there'd been no blood rings or dead eggs between them, as if she'd never told him to shut up and as if he never had. As if they were just plain old Millie and Sam.

"Do you want to grab something to eat?" said Sam as they approached the mini-mart.

"Sam, I'm sorry," said Millie. She stopped but didn't turn to go in quite yet.

"Forget about it," said Sam.

"No. I mean, I don't want to forget about it. I can't," she said. Because really, she couldn't. She wouldn't. She was done with dreaming up ways to pretend-fix their friendship. This was for real. "I've been really freaking out," she said, "and acting like some sort of wild, rabid chicken guard."

Sam looked at her and kind of shrugged and smiled. He did not disagree.

"I didn't trust you and I should have," said Millie. "Seriously. I freaked out and I'm super, duper sorry."

"It's OK," said Sam. "I think you just . . . you just really cared." Sam's voice cracked. Millie looked at him and couldn't tell if it was that cracking thing that happens to boys in seventh grade or if maybe he was crying a little bit. He looked older all of a sudden. He looked familiar but changed, his smile softer, his eyes brighter.

"I did. I did care," she said. "But I care about you, too." Millie didn't know why it had taken her so long to say this true and simple thing.

"Oh, yeah, no. I mean, that's what I meant," said Sam. "You care about . . . everything. I get that."

Millie nodded. She felt so much—so sorry, but so much love and relief, too—that she couldn't say anything more because it was almost too big for words.

"And you were right," said Sam. "I mean, look at how awesome that was today. That was so freaking awesome. That was worth everything. That was worth caring about."

It really was.

"Plus, Mills," he said, "I'm sorry, too. I can be way too much of a wisecracker. Everybody says so." And his voice squeaked again in that funny way, but this time he slipped into the store before Millie could figure out why.

As they passed the Acostas', both Sam and Millie turned their heads to look through the windows. There was a light on in there, but it didn't look magic or ghostly or even especially bright.

"So . . . what's the deal in there?" Sam said, as if it was a question he'd been meaning to ask her since the first day she'd shown it to him, way back before everything went wrong between them. "Y'know, with the light you were telling me about? And Lolo?"

"Oh, I don't know anymore," said Millie. "I watched it as carefully as I watched our eggs. Her light was always on. And then, one night, it went out. I think Lolo's gone, Sam. And the light was just me hoping. I wanted her to be in there—I wanted the light to be Lolo, or Lolo to be the light."

"Like, her spirit?" asked Sam.

"I guess so," said Millie. "But it felt alive to me. Like, really alive. It felt like Lolo was in there making light. But maybe it was just an ordinary lamp that can be turned on and off. Maybe it was no different than the heat lamp in our brooding box. Maybe it was never really Lolo at all."

They stared for a minute longer, and Millie didn't feel a pulse or a wave. She didn't hear a sound. Neither, she guessed, did Sam. So they kept walking past the house, but not in a hurried way. Millie was done with hiding and hurrying past everything, and Sam was tossing his can in the air, again, bouncing it off one elbow and then the other before catching it. Like always.

When they got to the Donallys' front yard, Sam said, "See you tomorrow, Millie."

"Yep, and if we're lucky, there'll be one last chick," said Millie.

"It's not all luck," said Sam. "We did it. We helped." He gave her a thumbs-up and a goofy face, and then he leaned in and hugged her, so quickly she barely realized what was happening.

"Um, yeah. OK," she said. And she hugged him back.

She knew he was right, but also? At that moment, she really *did* feel lucky.

"OK," he said, as he stepped back. And then he headed home, with his smile and his soda can and a wave back at Millie as she turned up the walk to her own front door.

As soon as she stepped inside the house, the dogs came crashing down the hall toward her and she could hear her mom chopping something in the kitchen. She felt happy and good about everything—Sam, the chicks, the yummy smell of cooking—but one tiny bit of her brain thought, Wait, why is Mom home?

"Mom, you are not going to believe . . ." Millie rushed in to tell her about the hatching, about what a *hen*-durance event it had been—ha, she smiled at that one—and then she stopped short. The fancy plates were out. There was music playing. Her mom wasn't wearing scrubs. Someone was coming to dinner.

"What's going on?" said Millie.

"I took a half day," said her mom. As if that's what Millie meant. Millie waited.

Her mom sighed. She bit her lip. "OK," she said. "We are going to do something brave and wonderful."

Oh. Oh, no, thought Millie. She'd had a lot of brave and wonderful for one day. Plenty, really. "Do you mean, my idea? Are we ... ?"

Her mom put down the knife and wiped her hands on the dish towel on the counter. "Yes. The Acostas are coming over for dinner. Because Millie, you were right. It's time for us to sit together. As families. To see each other. It is going to be ... hard, and it is going to be lovely."

This had been her own idea, Millie knew that. But she couldn't remember where it had come from or why she had ever thought to say it aloud. Her eyes burned. She didn't want to see the Acostas. It felt like all she'd been doing lately was seeing stuff. "Why tonight?" asked Millie.

"Well, why not?" said Mom. "It's time, and you were right, honey. We can do this."

In her mom's voice, Millie heard Sam's. And then, even more quietly, the whisper of her own. "OK," she said. "OK. We can."

And at six o'clock on the dot, the bell rang. Tess and Millie and Lucy stood at the end of the hall and watched their mom walk toward the door to flip on the porch light and welcome the Acostas into their home for the first time since that terrible stormy morning so many weeks ago. For one long, breath-held second, nobody said a word. Even the untrainable beasts shut up.

Chapter 30

Meg Donally was actually a really good cook. Most nights she was too tired or too busy to be a really good cook, but she was one. She liked food (unlike some people like Silver the Salad Eater), and so did her daughters.

So there they sat—the Donallys and the Acostas—eating a delicious shepherd's pie. Everyone was a little quiet but friendly and hungry, and Millie really did feel brave. Sam was right. She just cared about everything so, so much. But even still, she was brave enough to hatch chicks and say sorry to her best friend and sit with the Acostas eating shepherd's pie.

She was brave enough to care. Sometimes that made life almost impossibly hard, but also, maybe, worth living.

Finally, near the end of the night, when the girls had already cleared the table and their mom had poured coffee, and Tess had passed around a tray of lemon bars, Mrs. Acosta said, "Darling Millie..."

"Yes?" said Millie, and with that one "darling" she felt something dissolve in her—something that had been lodged in between her throat and her heart for a long, long time. She felt, in that moment, as Mrs. Acosta held her in her eyes, that she was a chick, pip, pip, pipping out of her own egg, out of her own black hole. She felt like the membrane had broken.

It wasn't over. She wasn't fully hatched. But she could breathe. She could look at Mrs. and Mr. Acosta, at her mom and sisters and dogs. She could see the light.

"I want you to know how much we've been thinking of you." Mrs. Acosta's eyes were full but clear, and they locked right on Millie's, but gently, in a way that made Millie want to stay put. And her voice . . . her voice was floaty and pretty and soft, just the way Millie remembered it from that night at their house so long ago, that night with Lolo. Mrs. Acosta's eyes and her voice and her hair and her dress, all so soft and so right. It was almost like nothing had changed, even though everything had.

Millie nodded and said, "I've been thinking about you, too. And Lolo. We've all really been thinking about Lolo." She said it loud and clear, and it felt good. It felt good to say it, to be the one to say it for her whole family, who nodded along. Mr. and Mrs. Acosta both smiled sadly in response, and Millie couldn't help but notice how beautiful they looked, smiling sadly, framed by the Donallys' kitchen window, glowing a little pink like the evening, holding each other's hands.

"Do you know what, Millie? This may sound silly to you, or a little crazy, but I sit in the rocking chair in Lolo's room every day now. I sit there to read and sing and think and dream—and I feel her there. Lolo. She's just there with me, you know? And when I look out the window, I feel other people there with us, too. People like you. People like all of you." Mrs. Acosta looked around the table at everyone. And then, in a heartbeat, she looked back at Millie, who understood right away and completely that the light had been on in Lolo's room because Mrs. Acosta was in there, being with Lolo. It was just a real and ordinary light, but also . . . it wasn't. It was magic and ghostly and godly. It was Mrs. Acosta's love for Lolo. It was bioluminescence, and maybe if Millie had kept looking for it after the storm, maybe if she hadn't given up, she would have seen that it had never really disappeared at all.

Mrs. Acosta went on. "It makes me feel better, knowing that we're all in this together, knowing that we all miss her so, so much, but also that we still have her in some shared way. I don't know . . . that probably doesn't make any sense to you . . ."

Everyone sat absolutely still—including Lucy, who was never, ever still. The coffee cups shone like little moons on the table, and Millie felt tears running down her face like rain.

"It does make sense," she said. "It makes perfect sense." Because it did. Millie had been right all along. The light was Lolo's. But it was also Mrs. Acosta's. And Mr. Acosta's. And even hers. Millie's.

Millie had become a black hole in these weeks since Lolo died—holding tight to the darkness, not letting even the littlest bit of light escape—and Mrs. Acosta was telling her it was OK to shine again, like she herself was shining, with Lolo's light.

It's what Sam had been trying to say, too, Millie realized. And her mom and dad and Ms. Fritz and Ms. Marion. Maybe even Deena the Family Therapist in her own maroon and bloopy way. But sometimes it takes time to crack through your own shell, through the shame and blame and grief of something, to finally see the truth.

"I'm so sorry, Mrs. Acosta," said Millie, finally and just like that. Not because she thought it was her fault, but because she was just so sad that it had happened at all.

"Oh, me too, Millie," said Mrs. Acosta. "Me too."

Millie stood up then, and walked around the table toward her—toward Lolo's mother—who wrapped her up with hair and blouse and breath, all warmth and light against Millie's tender skin, and together they cried. Together, they cracked open and made space for something new.

THE
END

Acknowledgments

This is a book about finding your way through grief, and like Millie, it took me some time. I am grateful to the many people who accompa- ॥ nied me along the way.

Lolo's Light got its embryonic start at the Vermont College of Fine Arts, where I'm lucky enough to serve on the faculty. It wasn't so much what anyone read or said that inspired this story, but rather the overwhelming creative energy and generosity of that community. I'd go so far as to call it a kind of light.

One of my daughters' teachers—Bobby Dan Harper at the Liberal Arts and Science Academy in Austin, Texas—regularly incubated eggs with his classes. He read a draft of this for scientific accuracy and talked to me about circuits and voltage and the percentage of healthy hatches, but he also reminded me how deeply teachers care about the humans who are their students. Thank you, Mr. Harper.

(Thank you, too, to my own fourth grade science teacher—Mr. Flores at Meadow Mountain Elementary in Avon, Colorado—who guided us through a hatching project that I've never forgotten, in part because of a chick the size of a rooster who rode home with me on the school bus. OK, he actually was a rooster.)

I had the most egg-ceptional readers and friends who helped turn this story over and over and over again, holding it up to the light as it grew into what it was meant to be. Thank you to Audrey Vernick, Martha Brockenbrough, Kathi Appelt, Anne Bustard, Susan Fletcher, and Lindsey Lane, to Chris Garton and Willa Scanlon, and to Kathleen

Clavey, who was my Chicagoan on the ground. You are the most faithful, loving, and careful teammates I could ever hope to be assigned.

My agent Erin Murphy built a heck of a brooding box with me and kept it warm for a lot longer than twenty-one days. I'm grateful for your faith and patience, Erin.

And honestly, nothing prepared me for the wide open heart of my editor Taylor Norman, at once Millie's mom, Ms. Fritz, Ms. Marion, Mrs. Acosta, and even Deena the Family Therapist (without the lipstick and bad suit). Thank you for speaking my language word for word and for seeing this all the way through to the hatching, even as you were doing your very own tending to life.

Thanks, too, to the whole team at Chronicle, including Amelia Mack, Jill Turney, Angie Kang, Mikayla Butchart, Lucy Medrich, Claire Fletcher, and Debra DeFord-Minerva, whose eggs-pertise made this book so much better and more beautiful than it was when I handed it over. Andie Krawczyk, Eva Zimmerman, Mary Duke, Anna-Lisa Sandstrum, and Carrie Gao, who all helped light its way into the world.

And if all that wasn't gift enough, one of my very best pals—Kathie Sever at Fort Lonesome—embroidered this gorgeous cover till it was absolutely luminescent.

Finally, and always, to Kirk, Finlay, and Willa Scanlon—forever cracking me open to all that is good and hopeful in life. I love you.

Liz Garton Scanlon is best known for her award-winning, bestselling picture books (*All the World* and *One Dark Bird*), and she also writes poetry and novels for young people (*The Great Good Summer*). Liz lives in Austin, Texas, and is on the faculty of the Vermont College of Fine Arts.